JUST A LITTLE SNACK

By Yah Yah Scholfield

Copyright © 2023 by Yah Yah Scholfield

Cover art by Amy Salomone
Editing by Celine Frohn
Back cover design & lettering by Charlie Bramald

ISBN 9781739511104 (paperback)
ISBN 9781739511111 (ebook)

Published by Nyx Publishing 2023
Sheffield, United Kingdom
www.nyxpublishing.com

For my nana, Lydia Coulson,
from who I inherited my warped mind

Contents

Just a Little Snack   9

In Which Two Women Kill a Man   27

What We Owe Each Other   37

What Dinah Knew   83

Suddenly, I See   107

Ain't No Grave   117

Something Got a Hold of Me   135

A Girl Walks Alone   155

Niecey's Garden   169

About the author   186

"We must not look at goblin men,
We must not eat their fruit.
Who knows upon what soil they fed,
Their hungry, thirsty roots?"

Goblin Market, Christina Rossetti

"No one can be sure of anything. Let them eat me,
I'll give them horrible indigestion."

Tender is the Flesh, Agustina Bazterrica

Just a Little Snack

Heather was so hungry, so infinitely and terribly hungry, she could eat—that was the problem, wasn't it? She could eat and eat and eat, and even after the last bite, there'd be room for something else.

Her hunger was shapeless, confused and confusing. It had to be the baby. Before she got pregnant, Heather had listened, dubious and amused, to the stories told by mothers. She couldn't believe it, the supposed all-consuming power of a clump of cells. How could a thing not yet the size of a lemon control someone so totally, make them want what they had never wanted before? It must've been something latent in the mothers themselves, Heather thought. How convenient to blame all lusts, all desires on a thing unseen! When it was *her* turn, she'd be stronger than the rest of them, feeding her baby only green things like dinosaur kale and rampion, spring onions and bok choy.

Reality set in around Heather's ninth week of pregnancy. The baby did not want what she wanted. *Refused* what she wanted. She spent the early months of pregnancy bent over toilets and trash cans, mouth bitter with bile. By the time the cravings came, Heather was too weak to fight them off.

Other mothers wanted pasta and cake and ice cream, cornstarch if they were desperate. Heather wanted texture, colors; the tacky side of a roll of duct tape, the yellow and porous flesh of a foam mattress, and, above all, Heather wanted meat.

She dreamed of it, drooled over it. Once, Heather missed thirty minutes of a prenatal yoga class ogling at a butcher's store front. It was all so seductive, the carcasses of pigs hanging open like empty coats, raw insides (ribs and rope sausages, butt and shoulder) spilling out of their slit bellies. She couldn't understand it; she'd been a devout vegetarian since high school, never so much as glancing at the meat section of the grocery store, and now she drooled over the thought of a single bite.

Heather tried talking to her obstetrician about her cravings, but nothing came of it. Dr. Ojo was an old family friend, avuncular and smiling even as he worked a gloved hand around her cervix.

"It's all quite normal, Mrs. Till," said Dr. Ojo. He slipped his hand out of her, slipped off his glove. The medical exam paper crinkled unpleasantly as Heather shifted, her backside gluey with sweat. She looked at Ojo through her open legs. "My daughter, all she wanted was ice, ice, ice." Ojo laughed, patted Heather's bare stomach, and Heather flinched. He sent her away with a prescription for iron pills and a sly suggestion to eat more beans.

Back in her car, Heather fumed. Easy for him to laugh and smile, to pat her belly and send her off like a fussy child. He didn't have this baby inside of him, this insatiable *thing* that wanted at all hours. Hot with frustration, blinking back tears, Heather removed her gloves.

Heather used to have lovely hands. Her mother always said she had dancer's hands, delicate and long, always soft and scented with lotion. Heather doubted her mother would fawn over her hands now. They were blistered, raw, the once dutifully manicured nails bitten down to the quick. Her cuticles were peeling away like onionskin. Heather brought her thumb to her mouth, grabbed a loose bit of skin, and pulled until it came away. The pain was secondary; her mind was empty as she stuck the wounded thumb, blood and all, into her mouth and sucked.

Maybe Heather hadn't been emphatic enough with the doctor? Next time, she'd come in how she felt, bare-faced and hysterical, gnashing her teeth. She was much too put together, too composed to take seriously, all reserved fury and suppressed emotion, her fury a knife pointed inward. Heather should've been honest, should've told Dr. Ojo about all the plaster she'd been eating, the pencil shavings, the paint chips, the strips of wallpaper ripped directly from the wall, the salty-sweet adhesive she lapped from the spines of books. She should've said how she crawled on all fours picking at carpet fiber, eating wood chips and hunks of charcoal, how she tore into household plants like so many potato chips. She should've mentioned, even in passing, the handfuls of dirt from her garden, the rolls of toilet paper, the glue sticks, the printer paper torn into digestible, fettucine-like strips.

It wasn't like Heather had anyone else she could talk to about these things. Her college friends (if they could be called friends) were not the sort of women Heather could be honest with. Her mother was neurotic, prone to nervous fits, and her sister, Diane, was notoriously self-centered, pompous and disdainful. Just the thought of trying to hold a conversation with her sister about her pregnancy was enough to heat Heather's face. She'd try to get in a word in edgewise, then everything would be about Diane, how easy her babies were, how dramatic Heather was, always making mountains out of molehills, malignant tumors out of benign warts.

There was her husband, maybe, but Heather discarded that idea as quickly as she picked it up. Darnell was sweet, good at many things, but bodies were beyond him. He was squeamish about flesh, and every change Heather underwent made him cringe. The few OB/GYN appointments he deigned to attend were awkward, Darnell twitching and squirming the whole time, frowning at her oily belly, staring with bare disgust at the creature growing inside Heather. It was all too much—her weak stomach, her swollen ankles, her varicose veins; they had agreed, even before she got pregnant, that Darnell would sit *outside* the delivery room, as he had neither the stomach nor the patience to labor alongside his wife.

So, she was alone. Motherhood was solitary, a one-woman act she performed to an audience of none. The eating, at least, kept her company. She made a game of it, seeing how much she could take, how much she could swallow before the baby got sick of it. Picky little animal cooking in her juices—it wanted bark and chalk, potter's soil, crunchy mothballs and curly loops of bar soap. Still reluctant to take the plunge into carnivory, Heather treated herself and her child to trips to the butcher's where they spent long hours watching the men turn whole animals into cuts, flanks.

*

It couldn't last forever. Eventually, around week twenty-two, Darnell caught on to Heather's less-than-wholesome eating habits. Caught her, literally, out in the garden,

Heather hunched over her flowerbed shoveling hand after hand of hydrangea petals into her mouth. She felt no shame, only bliss at the taste of green on her tongue, the sweetness of the petals. Felt like she was drinking spring, the stems she crushed between her teeth like so many sunflower seeds, the pollen making her saliva fragrant and heady. There had never been anything ugly about what she was doing until Darnell saw her, until he looked at her so coldly, more disgust than concern in his eyes.

For his sake, Heather tried weaning herself off her stranger cravings. She stopped visiting the butcher's window, ate greens and fruits, ate funny but acceptable combinations pregnant folk were expected to indulge in. She did as she was told, and if she could not longer stomach the sight, smell or taste of cooked things, well, that was no one's business but her own.

At Darnell's urging, she invited over her mother and sister. It was all so banal, the little sandwiches and stilted conversations, Mom and Diane cooing over Heather's ultrasounds. Heather dutifully answered their questions; yes, she wanted a baby shower. No, she didn't know the sex. Yes, she was sure Darnell wanted a boy, but she would be happy with whatever she got, so long as it was healthy.

"You really look so good, Heather," said her mother. "Look at your hair, your skin! And your nails! I bet your nails are lovely..."

Her mother started for her hands, to remove the gloves, and Heather pulled them away, pointedly ignoring Diane's sidelong look.

"You *are* glowing." Diane touched Heather's belly, and Heather let her, forcing her grimace into a smile. "Say, 'thank you, baby! Thank you for making me so pretty!'"

Smiling tightly, Heather said, "She gets her due, don't you worry."

"What? She's difficult?"

"Well, not exactly..."

"Oh, you're just like me when I was pregnant with you, Heather!" Her mother smiled, patted Heather's hand. "I was sick all the way through... Toxemia, you know. I spent most of my time in bed."

Heather shook her head emphatically. "No, Mommy, it's not as bad as that."

"Then, what is it?" asked Diane.

"It's just... Well, I..." Heather looked to her sister then her mother. She spread her hands across her stomach, pressed her lips into a flat line as she considered what to tell. "It's the cravings, that's all."

"*Cravings?*" scoffed Diane. "You're worried about *cravings?* Please, Heather, how bad can they be? *My* kids, you remember, Mom, all they wanted was rice and veggies. Bobby, I think he liked peach ice cream, but that was as funny as it got—"

"It's not that simple," Heather interrupted. She saw the look Diane gave their mother, tried to ignore it. "The baby's been wanting weird things. Bad things. Lately, I've been craving meat."

"Meat? Aren't you supposed to be a vegan or something?"

Annoyed by Diane's tone, her little glances, annoyed by the entire farce of the afternoon, Heather snapped, "I didn't say I ate any. I've just been wanting it is all. Thinking about it."

She didn't dare mention the state of her hands, the strips of skin she peeled from the back of her thighs, all the blood she drank from her wounds. Heather couldn't bear any more judgment; it was enough to be crushed by the silence of the room, enough to be watched and worried about. Heather wished she hadn't said anything. She wanted to bite something.

Finally, her mother spoke. "Heather, have you talked to Dr. Ojo about this?"

She nodded.

"And he said?"

"He said it was normal. Apparently, lots of pregnant people get cravings like this."

"Well, then," said Diane, clapping her hands together. "Well!"

Her mother cut Diane a sharp look then turned to

Heather, saying, "It's definitely stressful. Normal, yes, but stressful, nonetheless. You know, I used to eat clay, when I was pregnant with Diane. Mounds of it; I could've dug up all of Georgia and still have been hungry for it. I was too sick to eat much of anything with you, Heather, but I remember you wanted sushi." She chuckled. "Imagine that! A baby wanting something that could harm it. You were always like that, hungry for what you shouldn't have."

Her mother and sister left an hour later, the former with advice to keep in touch with Dr. Ojo and the latter with pointed remarks about prioritizing the safety of her child. Heather closed the door after them and returned to the living room to straighten up. She took the dishes to the kitchen, fluffed the throw pillows, and rearranged the home design magazines on the coffee table. She fiddled with the strings of corduroy on the sofa and centered a picture frame before Heather removed her glove and bit her left-hand pinky down to the knuckle.

*

And then there was Jameela. They met by chance, at Dr. Ojo's office, a couple of weeks after the finger incident. Heather was in the waiting room, flipping through a parenting magazine, holding her injured hand gingerly so as not to disturb the thick wad of gauze. Someone cleared their throat, and Heather glanced up and saw her, Jameela.

She hadn't changed much since college. Still the same narrow, brown face and eyes, the slender nose and high forehead, the thin mouth; the biggest difference was her massive belly tenting out her modish shift dress, Jameela's belly button obvious against the thin fabric.

Heather leaned forward, a little cautious of being perceived as overeager, and said, "Hi! You wouldn't happen to have gone to Spelman, would you? Class of '05? Jameela Hayes?"

The woman glanced up from her phone and searched Heather's face. After a moment, she widened her eyes, dropped her phone into her bag and said, "Oh my God! Heather Kilwin?"

"It's Till now, Heather Till, but yes."

"My God, it's been *forever*. And look at you, all knocked up and married! How've you been, girl?"

"Good, I've been good." Heather nodded to Jameela's stomach. "And what about you? How far along are you?"

Jameela crossed over to Heather's side of the waiting room and sat down next to her, angling herself so that their knees touched. Heather angled hers away. "Thirty-two weeks as of yesterday," said Jameela. "I'm having twins, if you can believe it. You?"

"Twenty-six, and just the one. Everyone's convinced it'll be a boy, but I don't know..."

"Who does? I'm letting these two be a surprise. So long as there's twenty toes and twenty fingers between them, right?" Jameela smiled, all pink gums and crooked, white teeth.

The women talked for a while, about their shared pregnancies, about their changing bodies and their lives since college. Heather mentioned Darnell, and Jameela mentioned she was going at motherhood alone.

"Really? No boyfriend, girlfriend? Nobody?"

"Well, not *nobody*. I have this amazing support system, here and back in Detroit. There's plenty of people doing it by themselves nowadays. It's all very modern."

Conscious for the first time of her plainness, her accountant husband and her bungalow with its stage home furniture, her housewife ambitions, Heather shifted the conversation back to their children. Jameela, for her part, was tactful. She prodded at Heather's sensitive spots, and, when Heather recoiled, she moved away without comment. Eventually, somehow, their conversation settled on food.

"Ugh! Seems like all I eat nowadays is meat, meat, meat! It used to be I just about *lived* at the KBBQ place by my place, but now I don't feel full unless I get some of the rare stuff." Jameela stared at her intently. "What about you, Heather? You been having cravings?"

Heather's cheeks darkened. Her hands twitched in her

lap. She tried to imagine Jameela with all that food in front of her, the folds of rare steak and pork, the pink cutlets of chicken. Her mouth watered. Inside her, her baby twisted and kicked.

Jameela narrowed her eyes. "My, my, my... Miss Vegetarian wants meat."

"I used to stand in front of the butcher's and watch them cut up the cows," Heather admitted. "I haven't had any, not really. And anyways, it's not good for me. Everyone says so."

"Bullshit," said Jameela. She waved her hand, waved off everyone. "Who's holding the baby, you or 'everybody'? What does Heather want? Beef shoulder? Baby back ribs?" She gave Heather a slow, appraising look from belly to hungry face, then broadened her smile. "Or are you like me, wanting something rarer? Sweetbreads, liver and kidney? Heart?"

Heather trembled. A thick globule of saliva fell from her parted lips and landed on her gauzed hand. Jameela threw back her head and laughed uproariously, clapping her hands together. Again, Heather was faced with that singular sense of shame, felt caught and seen; exposed. She wiped her mouth with the back of her hand, the action leaving a deep reddish stain against the gauze, and rose from her seat.

"Oh, no, don't leave! Don't!" Jameela took her arm and

guided Heather back down. "I'm sorry for teasing you. It's just... It's hard to imagine. Prim little Heather with her strict diet and neat little notebooks giddy over the thought of eating a heart." She spread her hands in surrender and said, "I'm not judging, really. Didn't you hear me going on about my barbeque? We got a lot in common, Heather. I could help you."

"I doubt it," said Heather.

"Why? We're in this together, aren't we? How about this? Next Wednesday, I'll come over, and bring a little meat for you to try. If you like it, great, I can always bring more. If you don't, well, at least you can say you tasted it."

"I don't know if that's a good idea."

"Oh, come on! What's the good of a craving if you don't indulge it? And think of the baby! This is what it wants, right? It can't be all that bad for you, if the baby wants it."

The receptionist called for Jameela, ending their talk. Jameela gathered her bag and her belly, and stood wobbling. "Think about it, alright?" Before disappearing into the exam room, Jameela winked over her shoulder and said, "Ain't nothing wrong with getting your fix, Heather. We'll make a glutton out of you yet."

*

Somewhere between the hour-long drive it took to get

home and the making of Darnell's dinner (Heather no longer pretended to eat anymore, could barely stomach the scented steam), Heather made her decision. She called Jameela after Darnell went to bed, whispering her address into the phone, checking over her shoulder to make sure her husband was still fast asleep.

That following Wednesday, Jameela was at her door, her silver Prius pulling into the driveway just moments after Darnell's car left it vacant. It was risky, almost insolent. The thought of the two of them crossing paths horrified Heather, though she wasn't sure why. Something about a crashing of the two worlds, Jameela's meat and pop music clashing with whatever productivity podcast Darnell had blaring in his Hyundai.

Heather stood on the porch, door propped open, as Jameela eased her way out of her car. She took her time coming up the garden path, touched Heather's flowers and lawn ornaments, oblivious to her anxious host. When she finally made it up the porch, she met Heather's gaze, grinned, and grabbed Heather into a hug.

It was all too much, Jameela's perfume and forwardness, the too-close sensation heightened by the rough weave of Jameela's dress. Still, Heather let herself be hugged, let her find some comfort in the way she and Jameela's bellies worked around each other.

When Jameela released her, Heather glanced at the

brown paper package she held in her hands. There it was then, the thing she'd been lusting after. Without a word, she opened the door further and invited Jameela inside.

Strange, seeing her house through the eyes of a near-stranger. The women she called friends, her mother and sister, they were all used to her decorating, her skillfully selected collection of art and furniture, the handwoven rugs she picked up from high-end design stores. They all expected the neatness of her living room, the vases on the mantle, the fresh flowers, and the plush off-white carpet religiously vacuumed.

Jameela, though, was a newcomer. She looked at Heather's things with a mixture of amusement and amazement, chuckling as she picked up the lithe African statues, the framed photographs of the Obamas gifted to them by Darnell's father.

"Wow. Just... wow," said Jameela as she walked through the living room. She made a beeline for the central sofa, eased down into it. Toying with the tassel of a throw pillow, she said, "All of this is so... *whoa*."

Heather hummed, pleased. She took a seat in the armchair across from Jameela, folded her hands in her lap. She glanced surreptitiously at the package which Jameela had placed on the coffee table.

They talked a little about college, though in truth Heather wasn't paying much attention. She didn't care to tell Jameela about the girls who'd gotten married, the ones who were successful and those who were plain. She didn't care about Jameela's friends back in Detroit or her family down south. The sight of the package drew her, distracted her. Heather smelled the blood, cool and congealed. What would it be like against her tongue, Heather wondered? Gelatinous, wiggling like jelly, or would it be as smooth and creamy as pudding?

"Heather?" Jameela tapped her knee. There was something in her eyes, knowing and patient, but eager too. Heather slipped her knee away. "Are you ready to eat?"

Heather nodded.

"We can go into the kitchen, if you want. I'll cut it thinner for you, easier bites."

She shook her head. "No, no, I want it whole."

Jameela widened her eyes, but said nothing else. For a moment, the women only looked at each other quietly. Embarrassed now, warm with wanting, stomach twisting, Heather did not know how to reach for the meat. She extended her hand, pulled it back. Flexed her fingers until the joints popped.

"Come on now, Heather. You're so close. Grab *it*."

"I can't..." But even as she said the words, Heather was picking up the brown package, turning it over in her hands. There were tears burning in her eyes, the baby twirling in her stomach. Her hands were shaking as she untwisted the twine that bound the package and pulled back the wax paper. She breathed out through her nose, drool pooling in her mouth.

How did she look? How strange and horrible, how unmoored from her sensibilities? If her husband could see her now, Heather was sure the shame would split her in two. Her mother would pity her, her sister would hate her, and all of them, all three of them would think such terrible, nasty things about her.

Heather looked towards Jameela sitting on the sofa, found her calm but curious face. What now, it seemed to ask. What will you do now?

Heather cleared her mind, cleared out her family and Dr. Ojo, her tidy house, all the motley things that kept her pinned in place like a butterfly under glass. She lifted the meat to her mouth, wax paper and blood and all, and bit.

In Which Two Women Kill a Man

Mr. Fillion was not a rich man nor was he well-bred. He had no land and certainly no lady had ever called him handsome. As a young man, he imagined it was a failing on his part, some flaw he could overcome with bouquets and sweet talk, but he grew and he learned the truth of it; there was no reasoning with an unreasonable society, no winning when one was predetermined to lose. Still, Fillion was no revolutionary. He had no interest in waving a banner, and cared little for politics. His gripes were personal, private. Unable or unwilling to dig at the roots of his frustration, he satisfied himself with plucking at the petals—women.

The problem was, thought Mr. Fillion, that there were too many women out there. Too many pretty things, too many girls blooming and blossoming, coming up like cosmos, batting their lashes, teasing their curls, laughing at nothing and everything and everyone. Much, much too many distinguished ladies, unobtainable ladies who scorned good, honest men and went for fops and dandies, who entertained anything with a pretty face so long as it came with money and land.

Ladies vexed him, hounded him. He loathed and loved them in equal measure, the resultant emotion settling in his belly like sludge. Sickened by their money (undeserved, unearned), their men (foppish, effeminate), Fillion watched from his shadows and stewed. Who were these creatures put on earth with him? How dare they be clean-faced and soft-handed? How dare they keep to their grand homes and carriages, how *dare* they recoil from him, as if his touch were something so vile? If he could, he'd wrap his hands around their swanny necks and squeeze the life from them. What justice! What a perfect gift it would be for Mr. Fillion to see those dazzling sapphires and emeralds *pop!* from their porcelain faces, baby-doll mouths gaping in surprise, legs kicking and kicking and—

But, of course, there was no getting to *those* girls, was there? They were too precious and watched over, kept in walled gardens like prize roses. Common folk, riff-raff such as himself, they weren't allowed to sully the petals, to crush the fine green stems with their grubby hands. The roses verboten, Fillion resigned himself to the quelling of daises, the flattening of dandelions. These were the weeds he was permitted, the scraps and leftovers, the wildflowers by the side of the road. These common plants, unremarkable flashes of yellow and pink on the street, in the alleyways;

Fillion plucked them by the handful. One and two and three, until his hands were red-washed and his temper was tempered.

Even now, sequestered in his execution chamber (a repurposed weaving house, tools of the trade shoved aside to make room for the tools of his death), Fillion couldn't understand why he was being punished. He had seen the scorn in the faces of others when confronted with his weeds, and he'd been careful to pick only the lowliest of them. His victims—if one could even imagine them as victims—were common girls, bastards or orphans, rough and busy farm girls and barmaids, fishwives and harlots. There were many of them in town, more than the world needed by Fillion's thinking. If one died or two, or five or seven, there would always be another born to replace her. He was only weeding.

Even so, they were killing him. Mr. Fillion wanted a hanging for himself, a good rowdy public show where he'd twitch and kick and claw at the rope around his neck, but the judge had taken one look at him and decided he was worth nothing more than a private execution. And, he learned, there was more punishment for him yet. Through whispers, Fillion learned he was to be executed by not a man, but a woman! What a cruel joke! All the havoc he'd wreaked, all the blood he had shed, and this was how they repaid him? With a woman's knife?

Fillion's frustration grew as he looked around what was meant to be his final room. The weaver's cottage was abandoned, the looms and stools and bolts of cloth pushed to the far corners of the room. From his position shackled to a wooden slab, room lit only by the sputtering light of a single gas lamp, Fillion saw little, but he could make out the shapes of two pails, a sword and a plain, woven basket. The walls were empty, the floor was nothing more than packed dirt; it surprised him that he was saddened by the plainness of it—his death chamber, the place he'd die, was no more decorated or fine than his own rented room.

Time passed, minutes into hours. The cold of the room raised goosebumps on his nude skin. Anger mellowed into annoyance then into apathy. He hoped his executioner would be along soon. He hoped she'd be terrified of him, terrified of *it*; the act of killing, the grim and joyless reality of taking a life. He wanted the whole affair to turn her delicate stomach, for her hands to tremble as she cut into him. There'd be no crowd to spur her on, no smelling salts to revive her if she fainted. A woman, thought Mr. Fillion, should be little more than paper, thin and easily torn. If he had to die by the hand of one of those creatures, let her be a waif. Let her arms quaver, let her lose her supper and fall silent at the sight of his black and brackish blood free-flowing over her white hands. If it must be a bitch, good God, let it be a mild one.

The woman that came for Fillion's head was no waif. She entered the weaver's cottage smiling, hearty and thick and flush with life. A stocky woman with big arms and legs, bright red apples for cheeks, breezed in alongside her. The two of them were caught in conversation, laughing, mouths open wide to reveal uneven, yellowed teeth. The women glanced at him briefly then paid him no mind.

"And I says to her, 'I ain't comin' back here if you won't give me by proper pay.' Miserable cow, she threw me out, right on the spot! All for askin' to be given what was mine!"

"Poor thing," said the hearty woman. Her voice was brassy, deep. "You'll take out on your own then?"

The other woman sighed, scratched her neck. "Maybe. Or maybe I'll find another bawd to mind me. You think I'll do well at Miss Marmie's place? She's fair, ain't she?"

They were loud, mindless of him as they washed their hands. Their skirts whispered against the dirt floor, and their hair whispered against their shoulders, mouths opening and closing wetly, kissing their teeth and clicking their tongues. The hearty woman picked up the sword and began sharpening it against a whetstone as she spoke.

It enraged Fillion, the noise of them, their brash voices and clucking, the sound of the skirts gossiping. He called out to them; mocked their gender, their dirty necks and mean, rough hands. Ugly cunts, hideous tramps, terrible lowly dandelions and bindweed and thistle, easy to pick, easier to trample, and just who did they think they were, ignoring a man like him?

The women glanced at him, then at each other, and laughed. The hearty woman, the one with her hand on the sword, said, "Is that anyway to talk to ladies? You apologize to Miss Tiffany and I!"

"*Apologize*? Apologize to cunts like you?" Heat cut through him, and Fillion thrashed against his slab, petulantly throwing his head back against the wood. He flexed his hands in his shackles, drawing the women's eyes, and they patiently watched as he clenched them into fists. "Think you're so mighty now, eh? Easy in 'ere, but out there? Out there, what are you but holes? *Me?* Me, I'm ante-fucking-diluvian. I've been killing weeds like you since the Garden, though God don't like to mention me, does he? I was born into world to make a rot of things like you."

The red-cheeked woman—Tiffany, he presumed—came to his side. Her hair was loose around her shoulders, and she wore a dress of gaudy blue and yellow. Her face was ugly, flat and covered with pox scars and spots. Still, there was an air of haughtiness to her, and the way she looked down at Mr. Fillion made him feel small and chided.

To combat the itchiness she'd planted under his skin, Fillion threw and twisted his body until the cloth that'd been covering his groin fell away. Bare, limp cock nestled in the wild bramble of his pubic hair, he grinned. He thought he might shock the girl, her being the younger of the two, but her face remained neutral. Bored.

"Really, Mr. Fillion, you might as well settle yourself. We'll take no more of this behavior."

Fillion recoiled. The nerve of this mangy minx, this *bitch*, reprimanding him as if he were nothing more than a child caught stealing treats. He cursed and cussed, and when he understood that words meant nothing to the women, he pulled at his chains. There was a moment where he thought he had the better of the women, but it lasted only seconds. The moment he tried to rise from his slab, the girl Tiffany cried out and slammed him back down, pinning him in place with her powerful arms even as he fought and scratched her. She *was* stronger than him, and it enraged him, her firm hands and marked face pulled into a grimace. When her strength began to flag, the hearty woman stepped in and pressed down on him with her full weight.

"Now that's enough of you!" Her hair came loose from its pins and she fixed it one-handedly, poorly, little strands of curly brown stuck to her cheeks. "Look at the state of you, cawing like a beldam, gnashing your teeth at us like some sort of devil! Shall we knock you about the head with an iron before we start, or will you behave yourself?"

Mr. Fillion glared at his executioner. She held his gaze, and in her eyes, he saw the Rice girl, the miller's daughter, the farmhand's sister, all the screaming chits he'd chased around the schoolyards and farmyards and into alleys, all the whores he'd backed into darkened corners or secluded places where no one would hear them cry. Worst of all, Fillion saw in her face the steady and unyielding resolve of a woman determined. She would not be shaken or flattened or frightened, would not be warped or torn or plucked. He was the cur, the bitch, the dog, and she was the dogcatcher.

There was nothing else to do for it. Mr. Fillion filled his mouth with as much gummy saliva as he could manage and spat it out onto the woman's face. The brown juice landed on her cheek, rolled down her dimpled chin, and plopped onto the floor. Behind her, Tiffany flinched.

"Miss Matilda!"

The hearty woman—Miss Matilda, then—wiped the remaining saliva off with the back of her hand. Gleam of spit on the hand, gleam of spit wetting her cheek, she called for her blade. "Be quick about it, girl. We wouldn't want to keep our friend Mr. Fillion waiting."

Fillion had wanted for the woman to kill him to be afraid of him, wanting her to be like the lives he'd snuffed out, temporal and meek, too nervous of his rage to fight him. Instead there was them, Tiffany and Matilda, red-cheeked and grimacing, sawing off his head with the single-minded focus of women accustomed to unpleasantness.

A plump hand gripped his hair while another smashed his face into the wooden slab. The stink of them—cheap soap and lye and perfume and sweat—singed the hairs of his nose. Fillion would scream if he could draw breath, if Tiffany wasn't bearing down on him like an iron, if Matilda wasn't drawing the sword across his throat as a viola player draws his bow. Fillion thrashed, and Matilda leaned forward into the fountain of his blood, teeth bared as arcs of scarlet painted her skin.

In the ten seconds between consciousness and death, Mr. Fillion took in his final sights, sounds. There was, for example, the wet crunch of his head coming away from his body and the thud of it hitting the ground. He rolled across the floor, watched his neck spill out blood like so much sap from a broken stem. He saw the heels of his killers, Miss Matilda's yellow stockings and pink skirts, and Tiffany's orange shoes dotted with pink spots. Miss Matilda, washed in red, still wielding the sword, lifted him by the hair. He opened his mouth but nothing came from it, no curse nor slur nor foul word. Plucked, uprooted, Mr. Fillion could only gawk at his executioners.

Duty done, Miss Matilda dropped Fillion's head into the basket. Both she and her girl were soaked to the skin in blood, and they'd need to wipe down before leaving the cottage. Matilda grimaced, set aside the sword and fell onto a stool.

"Will you really go to work for Marmie? She's not a bad woman. Nicer bawd than most. I know a few of her girls—I could put a word in for you, if you like?"

"Would you really?" Tiffany sat next to her, fanned herself with her hand. "I don't know what I was playin' at, thinkin' I could go out on me own. There's awful sorts out there, all kinds of men who might like to hurt a girl. Ain't that right, Mr. Fillion?"

Tiffany and Matilda shared a look, a laugh. The head of Mr. Fillion, discarded, said nothing.

What We Owe Each Other

This time when the phone rings, I pick up. You've been trying to get in touch with me for a while now. All throughout the day, all hours of the night, first thing in the morning, last thing before bed, the phone rings and rings and rings. Sometimes you give up. Sometimes you leave long, spiraling voice mails, angry and incomprehensible through the tears, but mostly you just beg me to pick up, pick up, *pick up Olive fuck please why won't you just—*

Sorry, by the way, for not answering sooner. The thought of talking to you made me sweat; I thought it might ruin me. I'm not sure why I picked up this time. Morbid curiosity, maybe. Poking the dead thing to see if it twitches.

You know what's funny? Before I pick up the landline, before you say even a single word, I know it's you on the other side. There are, surprisingly, other people in my life, people who might call around midnight, but I know it's not any of them. It's always been you, even when I've tried to forget. And I have forgotten so many things about back then, some willingly and some under duress, but Regina, I've never once forgotten you. Sometimes your face will float up to me in a dream, clear and unchanged. The baby fat of your cheeks, the somewhat impish curve of your lips—yes, I think I'd know you blindfolded, in death, every line and scar and beauty mark emblazoned on my mind like a brand.

"Hel-*looo*?"

You know, there's no one else in the world who has a voice like yours. It's breathy and slow and buoyant as the Atlantic. Do you remember your parents taking us to Myrtle Beach? We were in middle school, seventh of eighth grade. Your parents liked me, or rather they tolerated me always being around. Either way, I was your best friend and invited to tag along on your Spring Break vacation. The two of us spent the week on the beach, dusting sand off our Limited Too one pieces and spitting up saltwater. I remember it being my first time ever seeing the ocean. Beside it, I felt small and scared; I was a weak swimmer, accustomed to the chlorine-and-Band-Aid water of our local YMCA, and for some reason or another, I didn't quite trust the zit-faced lifeguard could actually save me in a crisis. You took my arm and taught me how to float. We held onto each other like otters, giggling and bobbing, staring up at the clearest, bluest sky either of us had ever seen.

After sixteen years of silence, your voice transports me back to the Atlantic. Limp, stomach clenched, and holding onto nothing but the landline, I listen for change and find none. Voices change with time; the vocal cords stiffen, the timbre is no longer youthful. I sound nothing like *I* used to, my voice gone gravelly and deep due to my nicotine dependency. You on the hand sound exactly the same. Just a single word, short on the "hell" and a long string of o's, and I can see you clear as day, strawberry blond, slim and ageless. I picture you a little older, just enough to suit all the time that's passed. I give you heaps of money and a penthouse far from our Podunk hometown, gorgeous clothes, and sleek Scandinavian furniture. In my mind, you're lounging in an armchair, idly swinging your long, tanned legs as you purr your finely curated collection of words as carefully as a hostage negotiator easing a gunman's trembling hand.

I wonder: which of us negotiates, which of us is hostage, and who's holding the gun?

"Regina?"

"The one and only. Did I wake you?"

You did, and I'm sure you know you did, but it's not totally your fault. My fiancé, Mitchell, thought it'd be cool to have old-fashioned landlines installed throughout the house. You wouldn't like Mitchell. He's not the sort of guy we liked back in the day, neither brawny nor slick. He's stocky, a short and pale-faced thinker with a goatee and a minor in philosophy. He spends his days writing think pieces and op-eds for online magazines, local publications. Mostly, he bemoans the sorry state of today's pop culture, how nothing is authentic and how everyone is disconnected. I can see you rolling your eyes, can practically hear you hissing into my ear that he's full of shit, just another pretentious, self-absorbed snob. You're right, of course. He's all those things and more, and to add insult to injury, my navel-gazing lover boy is a deep sleeper. Every time the phone rings, it's me and not him who has to get up and answer.

Not that you care, not that it's your problem. Suppressing a yawn, I say, "No, no, I was already up."

"Really? You pulling all-nighters, Ollie?"

"Blame college. Being a full-time student doesn't leave a lot of time for sleep."

You ask what I'm majoring in and make vague complimentary noises while I describe my academic career. I commend you for pretending to care about my major in ethics, for not yawning audibly when I say I'm studying for my doctorate and that I'm at the top of my class. I'm bubbling over with pride at the thought of all those letters and titles and accolades being attached to my name. For the briefest of moments, I expect you to congratulate me, but you say nothing. You make a flat, humming noise to mark your indifference, and cold oil spills down my spine, a greasy, orange feeling I haven't felt since high school.

I clear my throat, try to recover. "And what about you? What're you doing up so late?"

"Check the sky, night owl. There's a bad moon a'rising."

My body's taut as I rise from my chair and draw back the living room curtains. It's a blue-black night, bright with stars and brighter still with the hazy white light of a full moon. I yank the curtains closed and turn my back to the window.

Why do I bother playing these games? I knew, didn't I, from the moment you first rang, why you were calling me. I know you think that I've erased you from my life, Regina, but I haven't. I can't. My office is covered in moon charts; my phone is mostly astrology apps. I track the wax and wane of the moon as carefully as I track my menstrual cycle—twenty-nine days, give or take, for the full moon to rise, for the blood to flow.

I stagger back to chair and close my eyes. "Regina, I don't know why you're calling me about this."

"You don't?" You laugh, and the sound is ugly and strained. "Don't play dumb with me, Olive. You've never been a dumb girl."

I can't do what I think you're asking of me. I haven't thought about those times in almost two decades, and

41

though the memory is always in me, it's compartmentalized, packed into a box in the highest shelf of my mind. Those memories, the things I said and did, those are someone else's burden, the problems of a girl meaner than me, more cunning. To go back there, to ask me to take down the box and blow off the dust, to exhume the body, to return to her... God, Regina, how could you make me go back?

"I don't know what you want me to say," and then, "I can't do it. Whatever it is, whatever you want from me, I can't do it. I won't."

"Why not?" Your voice is encased in salt, unfriendly. "Too amoral? *Unethical?*"

Low blow, way below the belt, but I guess I deserve it. Shame floods me, red-hot and rank. Tears sting at my eyes and strain my chest, and a peach stone lodges in my throat, impossible to breathe around.

"Please don't make me do this, Regina. There has to be somebody else."

"You know there's nobody else, Ollie. There's never been anybody but you."

In the silence that follows, I hear sound from your side, and realize that there is no sleek furniture, no wine, no smooth jazz. There are only the sounds of a busy street, sirens, and wild dogs barking, howling. Are you calling me from a *payphone?*

"Listen, it's in a month, so you'll have time to prepare. One month, okay? I'm still at home, in Lawton. We can meet whenever and discuss the details, but I need you to come here. I can't do this one alone. It'll kill me to do this one alone."

"I'm nowhere near Lawton, Gina. I'm always, I'm..." In a whole new city. A whole new place, far away from my past, far from that high school and those woods and that small town where everyone knew everything.

"Then come back," you say. I hear the sadness in your voice, the tears pressing but not quite shed. "All these years, I've never asked you for anything. I never complained, never fought back, never wanted *anything* from you. Never said anything to anyone, not even then. I won't mention it now, if you want it like that. All I'm asking is for you to be here with me, *for* me. Please, Ollie, I can't do this without you."

Oh, how the mighty have fallen. Then I remember who it was who built your pedestal and knocked you from it, who led the crowd to trample you when you were already down.

"I'll be there," I say, and I mean it. I tell you we'll see each other soon. Before you hang up, you thank me profusely. You say you've never stopped caring for me, that I've always been your best friend in the entire world, that even through the worst of it, I was the greatest thing you had. I bite the inside of my cheek so hard that it bleeds.

43

When the line dies, I sit there listening to it beep. There's nothing else to say. No matter how much I try to twist and turn it, no matter how many times I bury that box and redact the records, I know and I remember; I owe you, Regina. Big time.

*

Be it my naturally closeted nature, shame, or a sisterly protectiveness over you, I choose not to tell Mitchell about us talking last night. I've told him some things about you—how we used to be friends, that I've been ignoring your calls for some reason or another. He thinks of you as your garden variety high school mean girl, a sort of harpy who, in turn, pecked at me and held me safe beneath the wing of your cheer skirt.

I don't change his mind. What'd be the point? It's not like the two of you will ever meet, and anyways, I like having a degree of separation between who I was then and who I am now. Mitchell doesn't get to know everything about me. I'm too heavy for him, my burdens like hundred-pound weights. If he tries to hold me, hold *us*, we'll both fall.

So, I carry it myself, all the things I've done and everything I know about you. Mitchell asks if you called again, and I say yes, but I don't say that I answered and promised to meet you in a month.

44

"She's a fucking stalker, Liv," Mitchell says. He pours himself coffee and leans against the counter. "I wish she'd take the hint and leave you the hell alone."

He doesn't know what he's saying, and I can't agree with him, but I nod anyways. I don't want to argue with him so early. I don't want to argue with him ever, actually, so I let him say that you're toxic and draining, and that the only way to deal with you is to cut you off entirely. You, o weeping girl in the phone booth, are a menace to my mental health, and until I learn to silence your cries for help, I'll never be at peace.

Mitchell crosses the room and puts his hands on my shoulders. "You gotta let her go. Sooner or later, you're gonna have to move on with your life, even if she's not ready to move on with hers."

What does he know? Pedantic, moralistic ass, how could he ever understand it, the ways that people change, how trauma changes them? I'm not who I was in high school. Those girls, me now and me then, we're night and fire, water and lithium. Mitchell's Olive is mature, charming and resourceful, trustworthy if a little secretive. She likes to be needed; she likes to help others. She's easy to describe and likes herself for it. She is simply Olive, ethics major, soon to be wife and PhD.

There is nothing simple about young Olive. She's vicious, mean; a wild and mercurial she-creature that lurks, still, somewhere within me. I try to be kind to her, try to understand why she did what she did, but she's not something easily studied or forgiven. She is hungry for attention, desperate for praise, desperate to be needed, wanted, watched. In my mind, young Olive is a rabid dog drenched in glitter and sweet pea body spray. I think at some point she might've been a very sweet little girl, very loving, but something happened, and she became this *thing*, more pom-pom and mindless ambition than human.

If I tell Mitchell the truth about you, about me, then I let him in on the secret of the girl I was. He can't know it, this thing we share. He can't know I was bad because then he'd try to console me, shrink my ugliness, hold my face in his hands and say that nobody's all good or all bad, especially not in high school. He'd wipe my tears and smile and say, "All kids are assholes, Liv. Their brains aren't even fully developed yet. Everybody changes."

Still, I know what I did.

Nothing can be done for the past. Our phone call weighs heavily on me, and I throw myself headlong into my studies so I won't have to think about it. I hole up in my office with coffee and microwave dinners, and write nonstop, scribbling letters to editors and essays I'll never publish. I leave the house only to attend debates, and listen with clenched teeth as others argue the merits of forgiveness and kindness, innate good and evil. I pretend to believe it when someone says that there's no such thing as evil, only ignorance and ignorant people, even when I know for a fact that true evil exists as a seventeen-year-old girl running through the woods.

I carry my cross, my studies and my theory. I think if I stop for even one second, I'll think of you shivering at a payphone, or in a hospital bed, or oh so alone, and how I put you in those places. So, I can't stop. I give up food, give up bathing. I give up joy and laughter and love. Mitchell reaches for me at night, and I cringe away from the feel of his skin against mine. I'm angry at myself, at him. Why won't he just let me work? Can't he see how important all of this is to me? Why won't he just let me suffer in peace?

After a week and a half of obsessive work and study, I'm yanked from my stupor by Andrea, a friend from college. You might like Andrea, I don't know. She's bubbly and excitable, a sweet girl, but she wouldn't have been in our crew. We would've mocked her earnestness, her stalwart individualism, her colorful hair and clothes. She says she's come to rehabilitate me, to pull me from my stinking study and out into the night. I sense that she's been sent by Mitchell, who is suspiciously absent when Andrea kidnaps me. Though I'm annoyed at being removed from my work, I have to give it to Mitchell for choosing Andrea for the job. She's good at these kinds of things—a hopeful social worker, she doesn't seem to mind getting her hands dirty.

Many others would've seen the sorry state of my office, smelled me, saw me poring over the same texts over and over, and would've let me be. She's not in the mood, they'd say, and they'd leave.

Andrea doesn't care what I'm in the mood for. She cares that I've been sitting in my filth for ten days straight without eating or drinking anything more nutritious than chips and soda. She cares that I've been lonely, that I've been obsessing over a ghost that none of my current friends know by name.

Perfumed and dressed for a night on the town, Andrea bullies me into the shower and brushes out my hair. She stuffs me into a pair of jeans and heels, wiggles me into a blouse, and fills a handbag with lipstick, my house keys, and my wallet. She spritzes me with perfume, makes me swish around some mouthwash, clips dangly earrings into my ears, and drags me out into the night.

We go out to eat, Andrea's treat. She orders food I have no intention of eating and watches me take bird-sized bites off each plate. I'm not thirsty (I'm parched, actually), but she orders several glasses of water and some ice teas and a bottle of wine for us to split. She waits until I've cleared at least two plates before leaning on her forearms and glaring at me.

"What's the matter with you?"

I shrug my shoulders. "Nothing. I'm fine."

Andrea scoffs, shakes her head. "No, you're not fine." She points at me and says, "*You* haven't left your house in over a week. The only time I see you is when you're sneaking in and out of debates. You were a mess when I saw you last Wednesday—that's not like you, Olive."

For some reason, this rankles me. How can she know what I'm like? What does she know about me, really, save for the miniscule slivers of information I've deigned to give away? I roll my eyes and pick at the edge of the table cloth. "It's really none of your business."

"None of my business?" Andrea falls back into her seat, brows raised in surprise or offense. After a moment of quiet, she leans back in, face shadowed by the dim overhead lighting and the candle she's positioned over. "We may not be *best* friends, Henley, but you're my friend and I'm yours. I guess I should've been keeping a closer eye on you. I forget, sometimes, that to have a friend, you have to be a friend." She spread out her hands, laying all her cards on the table, and sighs. "I'm trying to be a friend to you now, Olive. I'm trying to figure out how to help you out this funk because you're killing yourself."

In a small voice, I say, "I'm not killing myself."

"Then what's this?" She gestures to me, my slumped shoulders, the bags under my eyes. "What's wrong with you? Why are you acting so fucking weird?"

There's a bubble of feeling in my chest, tight and

49

horrible and about to burst. I want to cry. God, I want to cry, but I refuse to let Andrea see me crying. I never cry, not even in front of Mitchell, so how am I going to start boohooing in front of Andrea, who thinks I'm decent and put together and who's worried about me and who I've shown nothing but disdain ever since she came to pick me up? A tear falls onto the table, then another and another, until there's a soft gray spot on the tablecloth.

"You wouldn't understand. You *can't*."

"Try me."

She looks honest, earnest. Her eyes make me believe that she can really shoulder the weight of it. The burden's too heavy for Mitchell; he thinks too highly of me. But Andrea, this other woman, this person I've barely even registered as an ally, must know the way of little girls, how we can be sweet and sour, and difficult to parse. She looks at me, not as a saint or a sinner, but as a person—just a single person with faults, weak spots and strong points. Somebody who could hurt somebody else, if she wanted to.

So, I tell her. Sorry, Regina, if you wanted the past kept secret, the truth held forever in our teeth like cyanide capsules, but I tell Andrea about us. I emerge from the sea; I spit up salt and glitter and Victoria's Secret body spray, and I tell.

*

50

Once upon a time, we were girls together. We were like sisters, closer than close. As kids, we compared Barbie collections and played dress up in our moms' closets. I liked your house better than mine; the sheer amount of *stuff* you had intrigued me, and I enjoyed ogling at your parents (still married, mine were divorced), your toys (all new), your dad's home theater, and the built-in pool we played mermaids in.

Our dynamic changed sometime between elementary and middle school. Suddenly, I wanted: I wanted your house, your things, your confidence, your beauty, to be like you, to be better than you, to be you, to be with you and around you all at once. I was obsessed, and my obsession, part love and part worship and part hate, made me sullen. In middle school, I mimicked the way you dressed, talked, and walked. If you thought my fascination with you was weird, you didn't do anything about it. Maybe you liked having a less-pretty shadow that fawned over your every word. Maybe you didn't notice me at all.

High school was worse. You blossomed while I scrambled to keep up. People honestly liked you. Faculty, students, adults, kids; it didn't matter. You had a natural charisma that draw people in and knocked them flat, and everybody wanted a piece of you. You were student body president, captain of the cheer squad, and you won just about every title our school had to offer. Crowns and sashes and trophies and bouquets filled your bedroom as you collected accolades: Homecoming Queen, Winter Court Queen, Peppermint Princess, Spring Cotillion Princess. Your room was a shrine to you, all your accomplishments set up like votive candles at your light-up vanity.

And me. I was the friend, the other. I was proud of you, or I was jealous, or I was happy for you, or so miserably angry I could cry. You were everything that was wrong with society; you were pure perfection. You were the enemy, a split-tongued and lip-glossed viper; you were my best-est friend in the entire world, and there was nobody like you. I hated you, I loved you. I wanted to break you, embarrass you, smash your nose and break your straight, white teeth; I wanted to wear your skin like a cloak and crown myself with your flowing blond hair.

I got my chance, and you your comeuppance, on prom night. We dressed at your house, the two of us squealing at our reflections in your vanity mirror. Even with your monstrous collection of trophies and sashes, the hot-pink wallpaper you begged your dad to put up, your room was still a kid's room. There were stuffed animals piled high on your bed and an army of Barbie dolls posed in their boxes on your dresser. There were boy bands on the wall, a poster for a Disney movie; in one corner was the dollhouse you'd had since you were seven.

Earlier that day, your mom drove us to the beauty salon,

and we had sat side by side as we got our hair and nails done. We blushed at ourselves in the mirror, surprised and embarrassed by the little women we saw. We fawned over our big curls and French manicures, the makeup pancaked onto our faces by the aged beauticians.

We *were* very pretty. Of course, you were prettier than me, but I think I had a special sort of sparkle about me that night. I broke my piggy bank and took on extra babysitting jobs to afford a fluffy blue dress made of tulle and rhinestones; my earrings and bracelet were from my mom's box of costume jewelry, the shoes secondhand but clean. And then there was you, Regina, floating along with your soft curls, face beauteous with blushes and warm pinks, dressed in that cream-colored slip that haunts me still.

Shy of my dated dress, I laughed and said, a little unkindly, that you looked like Sissy Spacek in *Carrie*, moments before they trashed her with pig's blood. Tactfully, you laughed and swatted my arm. We looked happy in the pictures your dad took of us in the living room.

Andrea tells me she wasn't popular in high school. When she went to prom, she went with a small group of friends, then sneaked off to eat pizza because they were bored by the music. It wasn't like that for us. You were the It Girl, the princess, and I was your handmaiden, your lady-in-waiting. I remember stepping into the gymnasium, the light reflecting off the mirror ball blinding, the music too loud and too close and intoxicating. Our dates—a linebacker for me, the quarterback for you—brought us punch and cupcakes on dainty plastic plates, then danced us around the room to the Top 40. We spun in their arms, laughed when we made them blush and grinned at their jokes, which we felt we were too smart for.

Did you have a good time, before it all? You and your date were cute together, friendly at least, but I hardly knew my boy. I got the sense that you had talked the linebacker into asking me out, a sort of consolation prize for not being your first choice. My linebacker kept glancing at you from over my shoulder, paying attention to me only when I forced him to. He kept me at arm's length when we danced, complimented me stiffly. Nice hair, cool dress.

To no one's surprise, you and your quarterback were voted Prom King and Queen. The class president handed you a scepter, a crown, a deep purple sash, and a bouquet of blood-red roses. You waved to us from the stage, your loyal subjects, and I waved back at you with tears in my eyes, happy and angry and jealous, though I knew I had never been a contender.

With the formalities finished, the real fun began. You paraded yourself around the gym and teased the quarterback, teased the cheerleaders (not wholly congenial, but not quite mean enough to draw blood) for having lost to you. I smiled tightly. You let me hold your scepter for a while, and knighted my linebacker with it. Near ten, the football players decided that prom was lame, and that we should all ditch it to do something cool.

"Like what?" This was one of the minor cheerleaders, bottom row of the pyramid. She had acne scars that she hid with makeup and bottle-blond hair.

My linebacker suggested we go to the woods behind the school. "It'll be chill. Zach's got weed and beer in his truck." The zit on his chin, too small to see from far away, was glaringly red up close.

I looked to you for direction, waiting for you to pull back and mock his idea, but you smiled and said it might be fun. You told the boys we'd come out with them to the woods, that you were sick of all of this baby stuff.

I wasn't so sure. The football team's rowdy energy made me anxious, and the other cheerleaders were too lax and nervous of your disapproval to be of any help.

"Regina, no. We should probably just stay in the gym."

"Are you serious?" You saw I was. Frowning, you said, "Ollie, come on! Live a little!"

I protested, crossed my arms, said you were being gross and skanky, but under your mean and piercing gaze, I wilted. I got tired of being picked at, tired of the sidelong looks from the other cheerleaders, the sneers from the football players. I threw up my hands, and we were off, the ten of us slipping out the side exit and into the night, our only guides the strobes from the gym and the bright, full moon.

As expected, the "fun" in the woods wasn't all it was cracked up to be. It was boring, actually; a bunch of teenagers gathered around a slapdash fire, passing around cheap beer and smoking pot. The girls came out of their heels, the boys loosened their ties. You puffed at a blunt, pretending to be an aficionado, though I knew for a fact you bought into those D.A.R.E. campaigns wholeheartedly. As the night grew colder, your boy wrapped his jacket around your shoulders to protect you from the wind, and you curled in close to him, eyes red and full of moonlight.

We were too distracted to hear that first howl. It was faint, barely audible over the crackling fire and the boys' boisterous talk. One of the cheerleaders, the bottle-blond, sat at attention, whipped her head around, and asked, "Did you guys hear that?"

"Hear what?"

"That *sound!* That noise, it sounded like... I don't know, like a howl."

"A howl?" The quarterback laughed. "You afraid of the big bad wolf coming to get you?" He threw his head back and howled, and the rest of the team followed, howling and yipping like wild dogs.

"Stop it, Todd, I'm not kidding! I totally heard something!"

The boys kept howling and barking, and then we all heard it, the howling, high and terrible and too close for comfort. We stilled. The hair on the back of my neck stood at attention, and I peeked at you from the corner of my eye. You were gripping your date tightly, French tips digging into the meat of his bicep.

He laughed nervously. "Probably just somebody's dog."

"Go check," you said, nudging him with your shoulder. "Just go check it out. Please?"

You were always good at winning people over. A smile, a head tilt—the quarterback looked at each of us and summoned the courage to go. We all saw plainly how scared he was, how much he didn't want to go alone. In the end, he convinced the rest of the boys to go along with him. They went off into the trees. We girls were left by the fire, poking at the dying embers and picking at our nails. We couldn't drink anymore, and none of us had any taste for the seedy weed Zach's brother had brought back from college. You looked down at your baby-pink toes. I looked up at the sky and found Sirius, the Dog Star, winking at me.

How long did we sit in that clearing, thinking of fairy tales and wishing our dates would return? It couldn't have been that long. One moment it was quiet and calm, and the next, we heard running feet, someone yelling from the trees. We turned, expecting the boys jubilant and playful, a little out of breath from roughhousing. Instead, there was my linebacker with his white collared shirt torn to shreds, his face and chest a bloody mess, and a nasty gash across his throat.

Gurgling blood, he screamed, "Run!"

Shock kept us glued to our seats until he yelled again. We shot up from our logs and ran, screaming like banshees. Two girls went east, one went south, and you and I clung to each other and barreled west. Without our shoes, our manicured feet were beaten by the undergrowth, thorns and twigs and pebbles embedding themselves into our soles. Branches slapped at our arms and faces, yanked at our hair, and ripped our dresses. You lost your sash somewhere along the way, and your bouquet of roses scattered to the wind as we jumped a creek. I didn't know where we were or where we were going, but I held onto you and ran, breathless, until the only thing I felt was the wind in my face and the painful stitch in my side.

I tell Andrea how we were lost in the woods for hours, how we screamed ourselves hoarse in the hopes of being found. I tell her how we wandered in circles and found the bodies of the other football players, mauled beyond recognition, more meat than men. I tell her how you only recognized the quarterback by the scraps of purple sash caught in the pulp of his chest. I held your hair back when you vomited, dried your mouth and eyes with the bottom of my dress when you were through.

I see it now, the details clear as my own hand. There's the white moon, the scent of blood thick enough to taste.

I kept saying, "This isn't real, this isn't real, this isn't real," but my mantra was drowned out by the sound of low growling. You and I turned to one another; we already knew what we heard.

We turned in unison, and there it was—the monster, the wolf. It looked nothing like a normal wolf and nothing like the wolves we knew from fairy tales. It was worse; a hulking beast, all rippling muscles and elongated limbs, over seven feet tall on its bent hind legs. It stooped over as if its upper body was too heavy for it to support, and its long, curved claws scraped the ground. When it opened its mouth, we saw its yellow teeth dripping with blood, its gray-brown tongue. It stunk of blood, of carnage, and its eyes, amber yellow, watched us closely as we clung to one another.

I remember, because how can you forget being seventeen, hysterical with fear, piss running down your leg in rivulets as you beheld a thing out of your worst nightmares? How do you forget the need to scream, the terror that kept you bolted in place even as the monster lurched towards you? I thought that if I didn't move, it wouldn't see me, and if it didn't see me, it couldn't hurt me. The wolf circled us, sniffing at the hems of our dresses. It nosed your leg, and you whimpered, just once, and that was the end of you.

It happened fast. The beast lunged and you were flat on your back, scrambling to get away. By the light of the moon, I saw its teeth and claws sink into your flesh. It was a hideous noise, wet and hungry, the wolf devouring you with snarls and snuffles. I couldn't bear it. I did the only thing I could think to do; I ran.

I'm not sure what pushed me. Fear? Self-preservation? I wanted to live, and if living meant letting you die, so be it. As I ran through the woods, I heard you pleading for your life. You screamed no, you screamed stop. You begged and prayed until all your begging and praying became wet gurgling, then silence.

The lights were on when I got home. My mom was seated on the couch, worried sick and poised to lecture. How could I be so careless? Where was I, what happened to me? She took me in, the piss and blood and dirt. The shock was beginning to wear off, the adrenaline was beginning to fade. I thought about you in the woods, then I fell into her arms and wept.

"Olive? Olive, honey, what happened? What happened?"

I couldn't answer. I wouldn't answer. Who'd believe me? A teenage girl, a little drunk, a little stoned, babbling on about a monster in the woods; it sounded crazy in my own head. I couldn't let anybody else in, or they'd say I lost my mind.

Somehow, I convinced my mom not to call the police or take me to the hospital. She tended to my cuts in the bathroom and sent me to bed. The last thing I heard that night was her on the phone with my dad, whispering, "Something's happened to Olive at the prom. I don't... I don't know what to do."

The guilt might've been easier to manage if the story had ended there. If you had died in the woods, I could have gone on with my life. I could have lived as the friend who survived the vicious attack that stole your life. If you had died that night, I could have been the scared little girl, not yet seventeen, who did something stupid to save her neck.

You never did like letting people off easy, Regina.

You were back in school the following week like nothing had happened. You looked fine; a little bruised around the face and dressed much more modestly than I'd ever seen you, but alive. We didn't talk most of the day; I can admit, now, that I was avoiding you, too afraid to know what you might do or say if we were alone. I watched you from afar, trying to find meaning in the way you picked at your lunch and how you stiffened at even the most fleeting mention of the prom or the woods.

At the vigil for our missing classmates, we stood apart from one another. You were with your mother, staring blankly at a sea of candles and Beanie Babies, and I was with

61

what remained of the cheer squad, crying quietly over the quarterback and Zach and all the cheerleaders we'd never see again. On a whim, I said a few words for our fallen teammates. I caught your face in the crowd, wan and bloodless, drawn from a lack of sleep.

The Monday following the vigil, you sought me out. Right after gym, you caught me by the wrist and pulled me into the furthest shower stall, rucked up your T-shirt, and carefully peeled back the rust-colored gauze from your midsection to show me to the bite. It was my first (and last) time seeing it. It was worse than I ever expected, infected around the edges, puffy and oozing yellow pus from the puncture wounds. There was a sizable chunk of flesh missing from your side, and as you breathed heavily, new blood seeped from the gaping wound. It had a rotten smell, like sulfur and eggs and meat gone off. I swallowed the sick that rose up in my throat and turned my head so I wouldn't have to see any more of it.

"What the fuck happened?"

"My mom took me to the doctor. He said it was just a really bad dog bite. I had to get rabies shots in my stomach."

"Jesus."

When I turned back, you had the bite covered up again and were lowering your shirt. You leaned against the wet stall and wrapped your arms protectively around your stomach. "It wasn't a dog."

I felt the goosebumps rise on my arms, the hair on the back of my neck stand. Of course, I knew it wasn't a dog, rabid or otherwise. Even so, I shrugged and said, "What do you want me to say, Reggie?"

"I want you to say you saw it too."

"Say what? That we saw a werewolf?" I scoffed and shook my head. I didn't believe the words coming out of my mouth, but I didn't disbelieve them either. "This isn't *Twilight*, Reggie; those things aren't real. The doctor's probably right—you got bitten by somebody's crazy dog, and we were too messed up to realize it. You were drinking, right? And you smoked that shit from Zach's truck."

"That doesn't mean it didn't happen!" Your voice pitched higher, and some eyes traveled to where we stood. You pushed me further into the stall, slamming me into the tile. Cold water soaked the back of my gym shirt, and my head spun a little. Quietly, so that only I heard, you said, "Dogs don't do shit like that, Olive. You know that. You saw it too."

Rage swept through me. Why were you pulling me back into it? I'd just gotten out from under it, had just managed to figure out how to be okay again, and here you were, throwing me back. I pushed you as hard as I could. I hadn't wanted to go into the woods that night, hadn't wanted to be around the rowdy footballers with their cheap beer and weed, handsy and overexcited from the dance. It was your idea, your fault. I shoved you again, harder, and shouted, "I didn't see anything! You're a fucking psychopath, Regina!"

I left, stomping out of the shower stall with my face flushed hot. I couldn't breathe, and I didn't know if I was because I was furious or ashamed.

*

Andrea sits in stunned silence. Her mouth and eyes are red with tears. I spread my hands, unsure of how to move forward now that I've flayed myself.

When she finds her words, her voice is so low that I can hardly hear her over the din of the restaurant. "How could you? Why would you do that?"

I shrug, pressing my lips together. "I don't know. Revenge? Survival instincts? I thought I was being smart— playing the game."

"Have you told Mitchell any of this?"

"I can't. He wouldn't get it. It's too much, and he's..." My blubbering becomes full blown tears. "If he knew... If he knew I wasn't good, he wouldn't love me anymore."

I feel Andrea's eyes on me as I cry, and then I feel her hand covering my own. "I can't fix it, Andrea. I can't hold it all."

"Who's asking you to hold it by yourself? Let me hold some of it for you."

For the first time in the evening, I look at Andrea fully. She doesn't break our gaze, doesn't turn from me the way I would've if caught in the full force of someone's regard. There's no disgust in her eyes, no pity or disdain. I'm no smaller than I was before, but I am different and definitely changed.

*

Mitchell isn't pleased that I've been keeping secrets from him, nor is he thrilled at the idea of me going down south to see you. He sucks it up only because Andrea's coming along. Mitchell likes Andrea. He thinks she's sensible and honest; essentially, the perfect person to babysit his unstable fiancée. He hovers around Andrea's sedan, hands in his pockets, and watches as Andrea and I haul the last of our things into the trunk. I watch him wave goodbye from the passenger seat.

It's a six-hour drive from New York to Virginia, more than enough time for Andrea to go through the entirety of her road trip playlist and mine. I'm self-conscious about her hearing my weird mash-up of pop and electronica, but she's nice about everything, gently teasing me in the way close friends do for my taste in what she calls "drunk white girl music". When we stop to pee at a gas station in Baltimore, she buys the brand of chips I like and makes sure I eat more than the crumbs from the bottom of the bag. Andrea doesn't expect me to drive. Most of the ride down is quiet, not a single word between us, only cool air blowing through our braids and the morose moaning of this month's indie music darling spilling out from the car's speakers.

When we arrive in Lawton, I'm unsurprised to find that home hasn't changed much. It's as it always was, a boring little town squished between other boring little towns, the streets unimaginatively named after Confederate generals. The scenery's nice though, mountains on every side and trees as far as the eye can see. I ask Andrea to drive by the old high school, and she does so without complaint. We sit on the hood of her sedan and drink sodas while our fingers throb from the cold, talking about things unrelated to the past like her job and my thesis paper, which is winding out of control. Birds fly over our heads in V-formation, going south for the winter, and I watch their flight with more than a little jealousy.

From the school, we go to our lodgings, a bed-and-breakfast Andrea found through a friend of a friend. I call Mitchell to let him know we got in safe, then you, while Andrea checks us in. Stomach oily, hands sweaty, I listen to you tell me where we can meet. You don't stay on for long, and you sound out of breath, faint. I hang up feeling like I should've pulled you through the phone, and let you stand somewhere warm for a few minutes.

Our room is cozy; a queen-sized bed, two nightstands, a huge old-fashioned television set, a landline, and a small attached bathroom Andrea refers to as "quaint". Andrea sets her bags down on the right side of the bed, the closest to the window and the radiator, and apologizes in advance for her snoring.

I take the bathroom first, showering with the B&B's seashell-shaped soap and rinsing out my mouth before changing my clothes. I'm nervous about dressing up, worried about looking too nice and trying too hard. I think of you and me at the mall as teenagers, me trying on clothes and you shaking your head exasperatedly, whining about how nothing ever looked right on me. I fret over the cut of my jeans, my blouse, the expensive leather boots I've brought down from Brooklyn. Andrea watches me change in and out of things before finally picking me an outfit of the jeans that worried me, the boots and a purple turtleneck from her bag.

"You sure?" I look at myself in the mirror and tug at the hem of the shirt. "It's not too much?"

Andrea makes a face. "It's a turtleneck and jeans. You look fine."

I say nothing. I wipe off all my makeup, throw my box braids into a messy bun, and remove my jewelry.

We get to the meeting place before you, a trendy cafe on

Main Street. It's new but outfitted to look old, all exposed pipes and brick and heavy farming equipment just laying around. Andrea's a pro at these kinds of places. She leads me to a corner table by the front window then orders some kind of floral tea. I get coffee, plain, which I doctor with sugar and cream. Andrea glares at my non-meal until I order a chocolate muffin.

I wait, I people-watch. Maybe our little hometown has changed more than I thought. There's a whole new breed of people living here. Somehow, someway, Lawton's become a hip place to live, a meeting ground for intellectuals and artists too sensitive for the big city. I look at the girls in their graphic T-shirts and the boys in their flannel, and know that we would've bullied these people relentlessly. I think about Mitchell too, how he'd fit right in with them.

Mostly I think about you. About what you'll look like, how you'll be. Who are you?

You're late, of course. It's another hour before you finally get here, and the wait's made me jumpy. The bell jingles and I jerk my head up fast.

Let's see, there's a brunette leaving with her kid, a guy with a goatee holding the door open for them, and then... A woman covered from head to toe in ill-fitting clothes, barefaced and ragged, stands at the door with her hands in her pockets. She looks around, settles her gaze on me, and

68

smiles, revealing a mouth of yellowed teeth, the canines abnormally long.

No, *no*. This cannot be you. Really, it can't. All this time, I've been imagining you as the teenager I used to know, and I still expected her to come through the doors, not you. I wanted your hair to be silky and smooth, a gorgeous blond banner. I wanted your lips soft, your eyes bright. I wanted you to be devastatingly beautiful despite it all, but you're plain and tired. You limp into the café, chin held high but hesitant. You no longer smell like sweet pea and mixed berries, but like wet dog and musk, an animal funk that pervades the room. I wrinkle my nose before I can catch myself.

You come to our table and say, "Olive? Olive Henley?"

"Hi, Reggie."

And then you're dragging me out of my seat, hugging me, scarily thin arms wrapped around my neck and squeezing me tight. Unsure of what to do with my arms, cautious of touching you, I keep my hands to my sides. After a moment, I hug you back. You're too skinny, Regina. These are not the lean muscles of an athlete, whippet strong and powerful enough to jump, spring and fly through the air. This is hunger, your ribs against my full belly, bony fingers clutching at my shoulders. When I pull back to get a good look at you, I see the gauntness of your face, the heavy bags under your eyes, the sallow complexion. Still, there are faint traces of my Regina there, a little wit around the mouth.

You push your hair away from your face, bashful, then you catch sight of Andrea. I see you retreat into yourself, your face turning stony. "Who's this?"

"Oh, Regina, this is—"

Andrea stands and expends her hand out to you. "Andrea Perkins. Olive asked me to be here."

You don't shake her hand, which embarrasses me, but Andrea doesn't seem to mind. She sits back down and says, "It's nice to meet you, Regina. Olive has told me so much about you."

You snort. "You don't trust me alone, Ollie?"

I say, "You look pretty, Reg."

Cutting your eyes at me, you respond, "No. No, I do not." You drag a chair over from another table and settle it so you're positioned between me and Andrea. When a waitress comes over, you order a plain tea and spend the next few minutes ripping up napkins and rearranging sugar packets.

"So, what happens now?" Andrea looks between me and Regina, opening up the conversation.

"What happens now is Olive finds me food. It's three days tops, this full moon. I usually get by on two or three bodies spread out through the nights, but—"

"*Bodies?*" Andrea interrupts. "I'm sorry —you want Olive

70

to find you victims?"

You whip your head to Andrea, eyes narrowed. "I can't exactly live off *dog chow*, can I?" You exhale and look to me. "I need the blood, the meat. *Real* meat. I haven't eaten anything real in three moons—we're not supposed to go that long without it."

Quiet settles over our table long enough for the waitress to set down your tea. I watch you shake in a few sugar substitutes, then stir, the metal of the spoon scraping against the glass.

"Couldn't someone else do this for you? There must be others like you in town. Can't they get you what you need?"

The question *Why Olive?* lingers in the air like a bad smell. I can tell Andrea's aggravating you from the twitch in your jaw, the way you're tapping your spoon against your glass. I want to stand between you two, extinguish the fire before it starts.

"If you *must* know, I'm not exactly Miss Congeniality these days. I had a pack I used to run with, but they kicked me out. Bylaws violated, infighting, petty shit like that." You flash Andrea a nasty smile and say, "Like cheerleaders with claws and sharper teeth."

You're being mean and ugly, and I'm sure you know it. I frown and wonder if you'd be this snippy if it was just me and you at the table. I'd say it's not like you to behave like this, but it is—you've done worse to people you didn't like.

I'm only sorry Andrea is the recipient of your ire, the one who has to suffer that patented Regina 'tude.

I sit quietly as you tell us where you live (an abandoned apartment block near the woods), and what kind of *meat* you're looking for. Not too thin, lots of muscle, something with a bit of fight in it. You tell me that the unhoused offers a wide variety, that the more isolated a person is the easier it is to snap them up. I listen to this with bile on my tongue.

"It's not rocket science," you say. "I need someone to look after me, keep me fed, and you're the only person I really trust, Liv."

We finish our drinks and Andrea graciously pays for everything. You make a face behind her back, juvenile as ever, and it sort of makes me laugh. You hug me goodbye, say you've missed me *so* much, and then you're gone again.

Andrea and I sit in the cafe for a little while longer. I can tell she's got a lot to say, but my mind's too full to give her an opening. What am I doing here, Regina? You say I'm the only person you trust. Seriously? I think of how thin you are, how every clatter and sudden noise startled you, how you snapped and snarled at everything.

"I don't know if I can do this." I rub my face. "Andrea, I can't do this."

"We can leave, if you want. Something's definitely wrong with her." Andrea catches herself, flushes at her phrasing, then says, "She needs help. Not *your* help, per se.

A professional, someone who can, you know..."

"Fix her?"

"No, Olive, not fix." She sighs, runs a hand through her braids. "People aren't machines, they can't be fixed so easily. Regina's traumatized, very hurt, and some of her hurt has made her dangerous. I mean, she's asking you to find her *victims*. People to bite or eat or..." Andrea shakes her head. "What Regina needs now is someone qualified to give her the care and attention she needs to cope with what's happened to her."

"So, what? I let her starve? I hook her up with a psychiatrist and dip? Andrea, I can't do that. *I* fucked her up, *I* have to make this right."

Andrea furrows her brows, but says nothing else.

That night, I dream of you as a wolf. You're snarling, your yellow teeth gleaming in the dark like stars crowded together. You bite my flesh, and I let you. You tear my belly, my intestines spilling out and out, and I let it happen, apologizing to you all the while.

*

Do you know why I study ethics, Regina? My mother thinks it's because I want to be of use to humanity, to waste my people skills on philosophizing and writing research papers that no one will read. She thinks it's a waste of time, that

73

nobody needs anybody preaching to them about the merits and pitfalls of human nature. If I really want to be of use to society, she says, I'll abandon my lofty dreams, take up nursing like her, volunteer on the weekends, or join a church. My fiancé also thinks I want to make the world a better place with pithy quotes and lectures, become great and remembered like Aristotle and Plato and Kant.

They've got it all wrong. I'm not studying ethics to be of use, nor am I doing it to improve the human condition. I'm not concerned with philosophy or the distinctions between right and wrong. I know right and wrong well enough to know when I've done good and when I've done bad. I know the power of a lie, even a white one—I know what we owe each other.

Ethics, to put it simply, is my cross to bear. Some people crawl on rice or gravel. Others set themselves aflame. Others, still, self-flagellate, cat-o-nine tails leaving hideous trails of blood down their backs, their skin a map of misdeeds. Me? I read Kant, Book, Mill, and Stratton-Lake. I crucify myself on quotes from Locke and Plato—I go to my knees and crawl on the words of the ethicists before me so that I never, ever forget to cry for the girl I left for dead.

*

On the night of the full moon, Andrea and I dress in warm

clothes and head out to your place on the edge of town. We stop at the grocery store on the way there, Andrea buying a couple of bags' worth of raw beef, chicken and pork. They sit in the back of her car as we pull up to the abandoned building. A large sign warms people to be aware of wild dogs on the premises.

We walk the grounds until we find the building you described to us, then tramp up the concrete steps to your apartment. I knock on your door, jittery and cold, nervous of the howling I hear in the distance.

No answer. I knock again and again. I peer through the keyhole and see only darkness.

Andrea shifts the bags on her arms, shifts her weight from foot to foot. "Try calling maybe?"

I dial your number, and the line rings a few times. I hear your phone trilling inside the apartment and wonder why you're not answering me. I knock once more, certain that you're just in the back or in the shower. Andrea steps forward and nudges the door; it swings open.

I learn a lot walking through your apartment. I learn that that I don't know you anymore, even though once upon a time, you were like a sister to me. You've changed. I've changed you. I had thought, foolishly, that things weren't as bad as I'd imagined them to be, that you called me up here as a precaution, that we'd have one good talk and everything would be swept under the rug. I thought we'd forgive each other for all the harm we've done, and I'd invite you to my wedding, and everything would be rainbows and sunshine forever.

But here you were, alone in this squalor, alone in this unfurnished slum, living off blood and bad takeout. I can't see the ground for all the trash and clutter, and the air is rancid with the smell of mice and roaches, mold and stagnant water.

Andrea walks ahead of me, testing light switches before realizing there's no power and switching to her phone's flashlight. She peeks into the rooms as I stand in what might've been the living room. The desiccated remains of a possum lays at my feet.

I hear Andrea gasp. I hurry to where she is, at the far end of the narrow hall, but she yells at me to stay where I am.

"Don't! Don't come in here, Olive."

But I'm already shoving past her, pushing into what looks like your bedroom. There's no time to appreciate your decorating skills, all your old crowns and medals and sashes and trophies crowded around the bed, vases full of stagnant water and long-dead flowers. I would've paid more attention to the dollhouse laden with dust and the sweet pea body spray lingering in the air if it hadn't been for your body lying on the bed. You look stricken, eyes blown wide and mouth open in pain. I see the blood blooming from your chest, the gun cradled against your skin, burning the flesh of your hands and chest. The smells hits me all at once, perfume and blood and rotted, singed flesh.

I'm swaying on my feet. The world spins around me. Andrea grabs hold of my arm and forces me bodily out of your room then tells me to call someone. I dial 9-1-1 with shaky hands, but I can't describe what I've seen, your chest blasted open and oozing, your molten and charred hands.

Good play, Regina. Really, I mean it. Before I came here, before I knew what you were planning to do and before I saw your face, tired and defeated, I wondered which of us was the gunman and which of us was the negotiator.

A cop eases the gun from out of your hands. I guess we have our answer.

*

Only when we're back home in Brooklyn does Andrea grant me permission to read your suicide note. She thinks it'll be cathartic for me, and that there's enough distance between me and Virginia to keep prevent me from doing anything stupid.

Is it bad to say that I'm disappointed in the letter? It's not what I want; it's too short, barely a page long, and there's nothing in it about forgiveness or setting us free. You talk about being tired of hunting and running, tired of watching your humanity be torn from you moon after moon. You say this moon would've killed you, that you wanted to go out on your own terms having seen me one last time. You apologize for the mess.

Andrea's already read the letter, but I tell her about it anyway, falling apart all the while. Why didn't you let me go? Why could've you have written one measly line to exonerate me? Couldn't you have forgiven me? Couldn't you have said that you understood? Said that I was young and dumb, and that you would've done the same? Even if it wasn't true, couldn't you have lied, just this once?

I return to my misery, back to my studies, my hair-shirt of theory. A little tip from me to you, my dear Regina—never try to heal. It hurts too much, breaking the bone to set it, and we'll have to amputate it in the end anyway. Can we call it even, Reggie? And even if we aren't even, I can make it so by whipping myself for each year of silence, each cold look, each lie I told.

What woods? What wolf? What moon? What girl? Lash, lash, lash, lash! She's lying! *Crack!* She's crazy! *Crack!* You believe that psycho bitch? She's no friend of mine! *Crack! Crack! Crack!*

Oh, and you'll be pleased to know, Regina, that Mitchell and I are no longer an item. Turns out I was right! Not steady enough, not enough salt in my water; Mitchell drowned in all the bad I did. I ate the Olive he knew and loved, popped her into my mouth and chewed her up like my namesake. Another death, I guess. We'll carry the coffins of our past selves out to the old woods and burn them, a funeral pyre for a couple of former cheerleaders.

A month after your suicide, Andrea shows up at my place. She smells like tuberoses, body wash. Firmly but gently, she drags me out of bed and forces me into a shower, combs the tangles from my hair and does my face. I let myself be manhandled, stand quietly as she zips me into a dress and forces my feet into heels.

"I don't want to go anywhere loud," I whine as she clips on a bracelet. "I don't want people *looking* at me."

"No one's going to look at you." Andrea takes me by the elbow and leads me to her car. "We're going to an art gallery; a friend of mine has an exhibit."

Andrea drives us out to a huge modern building downtown that's brightly lit and swarming with people milling about with wine glasses, gawping at statues and photography, murmuring to themselves about texture and composition. Andrea stays with me for a few minutes, leading me to a few friends of hers and the artist. The artist herself is a sullen woman, hunched over and prematurely grey. When I ask about her influences, she looks at me with pure shock, like if hadn't occurred to her to be influenced by anything.

The artist brings me to a piece she's fond of—the focal

point of her exhibit. It's a wall washed black, covered in mirrors, and square gaps in frames that show the next room over. I stand in front of this wall of mirrors, and watch myself move fifty, sixty times. Some people in the next room see me and sometimes I see them. Some of the mirrors are cracked or scribbled on. The cluster I stand in are marked with quotes from ethicists and philosophers, a wall of judgments and moral proclamations all pointed directly at me.

"This is..."

"There's more," says the artist. I've lost Andrea, but I follow the artist to the next room where the wall is covered in words and it's the mirrors that are painted. Some are black, some are gray and others are blueish. The ones that catch my attention are the ones washed a somber blue. The artist presses something into my hand—a black marker.

"It's interactive. Write anything you want on the wall."

"Anything?" I say, stepping to the wall. I uncap the marker and cap it again. I can't think of anything poignant to say.

"It doesn't have to be *grand*," she says, sensing my apprehension. "It can be, you know, anything. A poem, a lyric, a joke. Someone wrote an interesting limerick in one of the corners. Dirty, but very funny. Something about vaginas in Virginia."

In the end, I don't write a lyric or a quote, a joke or a

limerick. I uncap the marker and write in small, cramped font *mea culpa, mea culpa, mea maxima culpa*. When I raise my head, I catch my reflection in one of the watery blue mirrors. The cheerleader that looks back at me is crying.

What Dinah Knew

Dinah's son was not her son, and it was only her that knew it.

Whatever it was that was wearing her son's face, it was good. A master impressionist, it managed to capture all of Orion's little idiosyncrasies, the minutest of his mannerisms. It spoke like Orion, moved like Orion. It even canted its head like her boy did, eyes narrowed in focus as he listened to her or to the wind cutting through the boxwoods, to the low drone of fat carpenter bees as they turned somersaults around the porch. The studied nature of its movements, perfectly mimicking her boy, was, at once, terrifying and impressive. She wondered how long it had taken to perfect those small details; the thumb milking, the gentle wheeze of his breath in sleep. Dinah wondered if such things came naturally to the creature, if stealing a face was as easy as stepping into a new pair of shoes.

Skill be damned, Dinah knew her boy and that thing, that horrible *thing* pretending to be him was not and would never be *her* baby. For nine tumultuous months, Dinah had held Orion in her belly, risking disease, fighting narrow hips and harrowing statistics, and braving strange looks for being such an elderly primigravida (she sniffed at this; she was only forty-one). She did not labor for nearly sixty-five hours, puffing and panting, screaming bloody murder, only to forget her first and only child. From the moment she saw him, she loved him, this beautiful boy, small and dark and red as a ripe cherry. Her blood was his blood, and vice versa. Dinah took him in, all of him, and remembered each and every detail, from the red port-wine stain spilling across his face to the fish-hook birthmark situated at his tailbone.

Dinah and Orion lived outside the city in a quiet, contained suburb on the cusp of poverty. The lawns were either scrubby or well-maintained, littered with trash or peppered with fragrant flowers. The houses varied little; they were all, mostly, brick-and-wood shotgun houses. There was crime, but it felt distant, the city sounds too far off to be of any concern to the neighborhood. Her neighbors were resourceful, friendly. Children were trusted to walk in groups, and blinds and doors were kept cracked, to keep an eye on the goings-on of the street.

Even so, those were strange and dangerous times. Dinah feared trigger-happy cops, gangs and street violence. There were whispers all throughout the city about a serial killer targeting Black children—there were at least eleven gone so far, missing or dead.

Orion was eight when he went missing. Dinah, anxious of losing her boy but refusing to keep him locked away, let him go to the park by himself. She sent him off with a kiss to the forehead, firm instructions to be home by six. Orion promised, but then six came and went without him. Six-thirty, seven o'clock, eight; Dinah watched the sky darken, watched the street lights come on.

The following morning, the neighborhood went into action, swelling around Dinah, each and every able person banding together to help her find her son. That first day, they combed the neighborhood and surrounding blocks, and, when it was clear this was no case of a child wandered off, they donned handmade T-shirts and scoured the woods, questioned strangers and known offenders. Finding APD unhelpful, Dinah scraped together money for out of state investigators, detectives. She'd grown accustomed to the sight of her boy's school photo in the morning and evening news, his goofy smile and sparkling eyes. His picture was on billboards, in newspapers, posted to the noticeboards of every nearby grocery store and further, plastered on the back of milk cartons, printed on T-shirts and flyers. Everywhere at once and nowhere at all, stapled to telephone poles, glued to fences and walls, Orion's poster called out, day and night, "Have you seen me? Do you know where I am?"

No one did. He was simply gone, unaccounted for, a white rabbit lost in the endless velvet of a magician's hat. It felt like magic, like a sleight of hand, Orion there one moment and gone the next. As days stretched into weeks stretched into months, Dinah's nightmares grew more and more morbid. Without his cheek to caress, his lingering milk scent, there was nothing to do but imagine. Imagine her boy mauled by strangers, by animals, attacked and hurt, crying out for her help. Was he stolen? Were they feeding him, whoever had him? Had he fallen into a ravine, broken his leg, were there leaves stuffed in his mouth, muffling his cries of distress? Or was it a stranger that took her boy, some dark-hearted monster who snatched her baby and deposited his broken body far, far away?

Dinah's imagination, vile and pitiless, granted her no peace. Dreams taunted her, memory spited, and after a while, Dinah stopped sleeping altogether. Why bother? The days and nights were all the same, monotonous and torturous, the lack of news as stifling as still air. Dinah came to hate the sound of the telephone and doorbell. She wanted no more strangers, no more pity and compassion, no more well-wishers and cards and flowers and stuffed bears, sorry-eyed people all apologetic but with nothing real to give her. She did not want gifts; she wanted Orion.

What cruel irony! For nine months of her life, Dinah

knew exactly where her son was. He was there, right beneath her heart, close enough for her to feel him hiccupping, sleeping, and turning. What sin was this punishment for, Dinah wondered? Did she want him too much, love him too entirely? If she hadn't doted on him, spoiled him, sheltered him, would Dinah have him still?

*

And then, just like that, Orion was back. Another sleight of hand, the rabbit reappeared from the darkness, her boy returned, wide-eyed and dazed, nine months later. Orion was scarred and smudged with dirt, but he was home and whole, physically if not mentally. The firefighter who brought Orion home said he was found wandering a public road not far from the park he disappeared from. He put Orion down feet-first onto Dinah's lawn, the boy's muddy feet and legs making him look like a tree suddenly sprouted.

Speechless, Dinah went to her boy, hardly believing her eyes. She touched his face, ran her hand over his coily hair, and smoothed her fingers over the port-wine stain. She smelled him—stale sweat and earth, that milk-and-powder scent she so loved. Finally, Dinah fell to her knees, grabbed him and brought him into her arms. She heard herself crying and laughing, unrestrained joy making her hysterical. She kissed Orion's face, his hands, wet his hair with her tears and held him close.

Orion made no noise. He let himself be held, let Dinah murmur over and over that she'd never, ever let him go.

A week after Orion's reappearance, there was a parade. They blocked off the street and decorated it with streamers and balloons, people from all over the city coming to see Dinah's miracle. If other children did not come home, if there were empty rooms and empty graves, at least here was one who returned.

A firetruck strewn with flowers escorted Orion up and down the streets, and a band played all of his favorite songs. For Orion, there were cakes and candy, pies and ice cream, enough sweets to rot his teeth ten times over. And there were toys, of course, so many of them—action figures and video games, basketballs and footballs and trading cards, thousands of presents wrapped in shiny paper and topped with bows of all colors.

Her boy would want for nothing, Dinah decided. Now that he was back, now that he was in her grasp again, he would live as a little prince, spoiled and kissed constantly. Time and time again, she swept him up in her arms and whispered to him how dearly she missed him, how happy he was to have her back with him. The boy only blinked and watched.

Deep inside, Dinah itched.

Life went on. Her child safe, Dinah went back to life as she knew it, working during the day and tending to her home at night. On weekends, she and Orion went to parks or to movies, to circuses and fairs and museums, to the zoo. She worried, some, about the boy not speaking, but she didn't think too hard about. He was still in shock, Dinah supposed, and it'd take years for the trauma of being separated, of being lost or stolen or whatever had happened to him, to wear off completely. Someday, they'd talk about it, and it could all be put behind them.

Still, *still*. There was times Dinah looked at her son and itched down in her soul, her mind tugging her someplace she didn't want to follow. Orion would look at her and blink slowly before curling up at her side. Her mind gestured; Dinah looked away.

The boy went to school and played with friends. At night, Dinah bathed Orion and noticed that the long, curving scar he got from the next door neighbor's holly bush was no longer on his left arm. Later, tucking him into bed, his port-wine stain was lighter than she remembered it being, and smaller. His eyes, too, were different. Before they were bright, dazzling; now they were flat and lightless, as dark and unpolished as the bark of a blackthorn tree.

I ain't in my right mind, thought Dinah. *I'm seeing things, making up stories.*

The following evening, she crept into Orion's bedroom.

It was cool here, the window propped open to let night air in. Dinah smelled pine and heard the call of night birds, cicadas and katydids. Carefully, she stepped over his scattered toys and the creaky spots in the wood that whined like babies when pressed. Dinah came to his bedside and got to her knees. She looked at him carefully now, taking in each of his features. Yes, this was her boy's face, his flat nose and full lips, his furrowed brow and soft wheeze. But she had come with a purpose, and she wouldn't be satisfied until she was sure.

Swallowing her discomfort, Dinah very gingerly rolled Orion onto his belly, raised the hem of his Spiderman T-shirt, and saw a smooth, unblemished back.

Dinah swayed and fell onto her backside with a heavy thump. The boy turned over then, wooden eyes quickly finding her in the dark. He yawned, but when he spoke his voice was clear. He said, "Mama?"

Dinah shook her head, stumbled to her feet, and half-ran, half-tripped out of the room. In the bathroom, she collapsed over the toilet and voided her stomach. Her head was pounding; she rested it against the porcelain rim, inhaling and exhaling shaky breaths that neither helped nor soothed. She wanted to scream, wanted to beat her chest and cry out, "Why me? Why me?"

Then again, why not her and who else? The boy's father wanted nothing to do with him, and Dinah was the only family Orion had. Who else would care about or notice Orion's changes? Who else would take note of the little differences that separated her child from an imposter? Others might've let it go, taken this replacement child without so much as another thought, but Dinah was not others. She was and could only be herself, too smart for her own good and too sensitive, a mother who couldn't be a sucker for anyone, not even for herself.

Now that Dinah knew, she couldn't sleep. She sat down at the kitchen table and wrote out a long list of things she knew to be true, things that were immutable. Her name was Dinah, she lived in Atlanta, Georgia, and she was forty-nine years old. She had a son called Orion, and ten months ago that son went missing. Dinah never learned who or what took him, where he had been or what happened to him while he was away. All she had was what the fireman told her, that the boy was found in the woods prodding at a bug in his usual fashion, calm and unscathed if dirty. The boy with the stick was not the boy she birthed. Dinah had to consider now—if not her child, then whose? If not her boy, then what?

She wrote her theories down as she thought them, giving them each a moment then discarding those she didn't find likely. There were countless missing children in Atlanta at the moment, enough Black kids to be misidentified, swapped and placed in wrong homes, wrong graves. How many disappeared children were the same height and color as Orion, who wore the same brand of clothes and shoes? It was possible that the boy in her house was another woman's son, and that *that* woman had hers. Then, too, the boy could've been homeless, a little urchin passing through town who found himself at the right place at the right time. That happened sometimes, right? Vagrants looking for homes, snapping into the nearest and most convenient place like puzzle pieces from disparate sets—a velvety pink cat ear in the midst of a cityscape, bright scrap of river interrupting a log cabin.

Maybe he isn't a boy at all, supplied Dinah's mind. A mean itch started up her legs, burning like fire ants. *Maybe he ain't even human.*

Dinah laughed aloud at the thought. It was the dumbest idea she'd had all evening, and she would've gone hot in the face if anybody heard her say it. Dinah didn't hold with a lot of superstition. Sure, she threw salt over her shoulder and never whistled indoors, painted her front door blue and knocked on wood, but faeries were a little much for her. Faeries were for children, gossamer wings and tinkling bells to amuse babies. Dinah snorted and laughed again, but the laughter dried up. She gnawed on the inside of her cheek.

Of course, Dinah had heard stories. Nowadays, everyone agreed that they were silly, but still the stories persevered and were passed from parent to parent. Sasha from down the street was said to have lost a baby sister in that way. Her mother left the bedroom window open, and come morning, the child was gone, replaced with a pair of kitchen scissors. The grandmother-tales about children being taken, swapped, switched and stolen; the stories told by her friends, some giggling and some deadly serious, about mossy hands grabbing the meat of babies' arms, pinching their fatty cheeks and prodding at them as if picking over ripe fruit. And then, most damning, what Dinah knew herself, her own sister who wasn't quite right, who was rumored to have been a block of wood. Wasn't it just a little bit likely that all of those faery tales contained grains of truth? Wasn't it possible that her boy was a changeling?

Dinah threw down her notepad and pencil, and pressed the pads of her fingers into her eyes until she saw colors. A clattering sound from behind startled her, and she turned. The boy was there, clutching Orion's teddy bear and rubbing at his strange eyes with the back of his hand.

"Mama?"

*

To know what had become of Orion, we must become the trees. See now from the view of a sentinel, wise and without age, the tranquil peace of a spring afternoon. The park was in full bloom, fresh and verdant, the smell of the tall fescue grass heady. Bees somersaulted through the heads of dandelions and hornets swept low over the grass, depositing their pollen. Everywhere, there was a low, barely audible hum of cicadas and katydids.

There was a playground at the park, but it was mostly defunct, rusted away and occupied by older kids. Regardless, the boy preferred his own game and company. He rolled around in the tall grass, dragging trucks and action figures through the dirt. He flew cars and boats around phone poles, ran in wild circles around and around the park until he was dizzy. The boy examined the paths of ants, cautiously but curiously studied the flight pattern of the bees, and mimicked a grasshopper until he was thoroughly bored.

What else could he do? He wasn't supposed to wander off from the park, and he had promised his mom he'd be home before six. Sighing, the boy laid out on the grass in a star, arms and legs splayed wide. He looked up into the cloudless blue sky. The trees covered him, their thoughts as deep and contemplative as his own.

Nature, mother to everything and nothing, cared little for what belonged to this or that creature. The trees sent flashes of light down through their leaves, canting the sun in all directions, and threw out bright will-o'-the-wisps onto the bushes and branches to catch the boy's attention.

Upon seeing them, the boy's eyes widened. He crept to the lights slowly at first, and then sprinted after them. He thought, maybe, that he'd be back in time for dinner. The trees made no promises, only led him further into the woods with their light-tricks, past a twisted wire fence and through a patch of stinging nettle. On hands and knees, the boy crawled through thorns and prickly bushes until he was in the forest, surrounded by buckeye and myrtle bushes. He chased the wisps as they danced past him, laughing and grabbing at them with his hands. The boy fell onto the grass, rolling and squealing, enamored with the feeling of pure light in his fingers.

The trees observed. It was difficult to lure in a full-grown person, their minds not so accepting of the fantastic, but with children it was simple. They saw the woods as the boy did then, through enchanted eyes. Dewdrops hung from the tips of leaves like crystals, and over-ripened berries stained the undergrowth purple. The air was sweet with the scent of pine needle and jasmine. Pale sunlight filtered in through the thick boxwood canopy, patterning his brown skin with round, leafy shapes. Sometimes, the boy stopped his play and fell silent, reverent in the midst of birdsong and whispering wind, the low hum of insects.

He was a good one, thought the trees. Some of the human children were not so nice. They were destructive, careless, but this one was so gentle and mild-mannered, and curious above all else. The trees led him in deeper and deeper, until the boy stood in a lush valley of flowers and mushrooms. All around him, as far as the eye could see, were dog-violets, peonies, fringed blue star and white baneberry, white and red mushrooms, and toadstools big enough to sit on. The boy ran his hands over the flowers and patted the soft, squishy heads of fungi. He'd never seen such a thing before. Such idyllic beauty existed only in storybooks, and the trees liked it that way. Innocence was the best trait in times such as these. The children expected nothing and wanted everything, their minds as receptive as thirsty roots.

The boy was not without company. As he lazed in the valley, one of the magnolias bent low and changed shape to call herself she. She came to him and touched his forehead, and smiled in a way she thought might be comforting to a human child.

The boy, cautious of strangers but remembering his mother's lessons in manners, smiled back and said, "Hello!"

"Hello, Orion!"

If the boy thought it was odd that the stranger knew his name, he did not hold the thought for long. She offered him her hand, and he took it, and the two of them walked together for a while, deeper into the woods, to a cottage she called her home. The boy liked the look of the house, how white and majestic it was, how there was a big porch and a garden greener and grander than his mother's. The boy looked the woman over. He supposed she looked like his mother as well, just a little, though she seemed less exhausted than his mother.

As if hearing his thoughts, the lady said, "Let's play a game!"

They played tag and hide-and-seek, four corners and mother-may-I. She showed him magic tricks—not the phony kind with cards and flowers, but the real sort with faeries being formed from leaves, rocks being coins to purchase tinctures of rainwater.

When the boy grew tired, the lady offered him a place to sleep. The boy looked over his shoulder, thinking of his mother. Beseechingly, the lady said, "Come on, Orion! Don't you want to keep playing pretend?"

He didn't know how to say no to her, and besides, the place looked nice enough. The lady led him to the house and offered him food. Onto the table, she piled cakes and candy, tarts and pies and sweet creams, soft rolls filled with jam, others with butter and sugar, cinnamon and honey. The boy ate until his stomach ached, no longer hungry but unable to stop, the lady's bright eyes pinning him into place. She watched him as he chewed, smiling broadly, her chin propped up on her hand.

The boy shook his head. "I can't eat any more."

"No? Do you have a tummy ache?"

The boy nodded, and the lady rose to her feet. She went to a cabinet, took out two mismatched cups and a tall pitcher filled with pale green water. She poured him a cupful, and bade the boy to drink it, the twigs and leaves and flower petals and all. The boy shied away, suspicious of the floating things and strange color. The lady, thinking that the human child didn't know how to take the drink, demonstrated, tilting back her head and pouring the water into her mouth. She rubbed her belly and hummed, smiled toothily.

An adult's reassurance was good enough for the boy. Orion drank what was in his cup, then drank more and more as the lady filled and refilled his cup. By the time the pitcher was empty, the boy was languid, eyelids heavy and his limbs even heavier. His tongue was thick and uncomfortable in his mouth, and his mind was dull, nearly still.

"I don't think I feel well," said the boy. He clutched his stomach and curled in on himself.

The lady cooed. "Poor thing, poor baby." She picked him up and nestled him close to her chest, rocking him as softly as a newborn. "You need rest. Doesn't it sound good to rest?"

The boy didn't know. He wanted his mother, but he couldn't find the words to call for her. He went limp in the lady's arms, his consciousness waning as she undressed him and draped him with tree bark, with leaves. She placed a bird's nest on his head, and tied a cape of lichen around his small shoulders. The lady lifted him out of his sneakers and planted him down in her garden, feet first, and packed the dirt down tight. The boy's mind drifted, unmoored itself. The lady raised his arms high over his head. A bee landed on the boy's cheek.

The trees swayed in unison. Another one there, another one to join their numbers. The sequoia took her place beside the boy, just a magnolia sapling.

Elsewhere, standing out on her lawn full of abandoned toys, the mother called for her son. He answered her without words, wind and the smell of magnolias from miles away.

*

There was no easy way to be rid of the changeling. Other people called it her son, so it had to be Orion for the time being. Lord knew, Dinah didn't want him. How could she? Somewhere out there, her true son was waiting for her. She needed to leave a space open for him, leave room in her heart like a porchlight in the dark.

Dinah had a theory. She thought, maybe, that there was only so much space in the universe for so many, and that these slots, preordained, belong to certain people. As long as the changeling stood in Orion's place, her boy couldn't come home. If he were gone again, gone back to whatever crucible he was formed in, the universe would balance itself out. Something lost and something retrieved, something taken and something else, quickly and mistakenly, replacing it. If only that thing would go, if only her boy would come back...

Time passed. Weeks became months, months became a year. Dinah's hope waned. Be he alive or be he dead, Dinah wanted her child. If she couldn't have him young and whole, then damnit, she wanted his bones to weep over, what little remained of his flesh and clothes to bury. Two years passed, the Atlanta killer was caught and arrested; the arrest didn't resurrect the dead, but it made for nice TV, the end of an era of fear. The changeling turned ten, then eleven and twelve. Dinah looked into its wooden eyes and tried to forgive the coloring of the port-wine stain. Maybe she could replicate the scar on his arm?

It wasn't easy work, making room within herself for the not-Orion. The boy also struggled; what was obvious to Dinah—his oddities, his lack of belonging—was obvious to his peers as well. Both mother and creature ended their days in something of a confused exhaustion. Every evening, Dinah tucked the boy into bed, eyes cataloging each new bruise and scar.

"What happened here?" Dinah asked, fingers glancing

off a jagged scar over the boy's eye.

"They pushed me," he said quietly. He gave no more information on who *they* were, these faceless, shoving children, nor did Dinah want any. She imagined them to be boys from the neighborhood, former friends of Orion's turned adversaries.

Dinah made a noncommittal noise. "That's how it is here," she told him. "People see things that don't fit, they try pushing it out." She felt the meanness rise up in her, mouth curling as it filled with poison. "My boy, he never have a problem with nobody, now you come. Might be easier, don't you think, going back to where you belong?"

She glanced down at the boy and was surprised to find his eyes glazed with tears. His chest worked up and down, mouth twisting to hold back a sob. A cold, oily feeling fell over Dinah. Unsure of what to do with it, she patted the boy's hand and left the room, her own chest tight with shame.

Shame for what, Dinah wondered? For honesty? Shame for telling the thing the truth of how she felt? Dinah knew it was something simpler. She'd never talked to her Orion like that, never rose her hand or voice, never said anything to him that'd make his face fall so. And even if the boy lying in her son's bed wasn't hers, per se, it was still a boy, still a child that cried when it was insulted and suffered bruises and cruelty. Dinah could only hope that whatever thing

101

held her son was kinder to him than she was to the creature.

Come morning, there was a full breakfast waiting for the changeling—pancakes, eggs, bacon, all of Orion's favorites. What Dinah couldn't say with words, she said with a healthy pour of maple syrup and a light touch to the boy's curly head.

Dinah was gentler with the boy from then on. More often than not, she came rushing to the boy's defense, the chest tightening rage she felt on his behalf a shock. She made concessions, drew new lines in the sand. After a while, Dinah stopped looking for signs of her first Orion in the changeling and took what she was given. She taught him things, gave him Orion's memories and favorites. This is how you take your eggs, she said to him. This is the music that you like, the way you dance, the way you smile at me. In turn, the changeling gifted Dinah a new birthmark, a cherry-colored splotch on his lower back, more question mark than fishhook.

Like any child, he aged, becoming the person her boy might've grown into, if he'd been allowed to age. When the changeling turned fifteen, Dinah laid down new rules. A truce of sorts, so they both knew where they stood and what lines couldn't be crossed. Dinah allowed the boy to call her 'mother' in public and nowhere else. At home, he wasn't to touch her, call her, need her. She was his temporary caretaker and nothing more. When he became a man, he could do whatever he pleased, so long as he left her be.

"We not gonna play no silly games with each other," said Dinah, and the changeling agreed. They knew the truth, Dinah and this creature, and it wouldn't be right to be cruel to one another. It was only fair to keep empty the spaces neither of them could truthfully occupy.

At age seventeen, the changeling called her 'ma' in a soft, teasing voice. Dinah fought the urge to slap the thing across its face. Nine years had gone and hearing that name on his lips still felt like a taunt. She took in a slow breath. Tears dripped down her chin, and a clear line of snot laid down over her top lip. Dinah thought of her boy, surely dead by now, surely rotted away to nothing, more bone than flesh.

The changeling touched her wet cheek gently, not unlike how she used to soothe him before she knew the truth. "Mama?"

Her chest ached. Dinah nodded, covered Orion's hand with hers and found that she loved it.

*

The changeling didn't immediately leave when he was grown like Dinah thought he would. He stayed with her, right beside her, as she worked and tended to her home, offering sometimes to help but mostly just sitting near, canting his head and narrowing his eyes to hear her better.

The changeling went to college, then found a place of his own. He came to visit her often, content to sit at her feet and tell her stories about his life before her. Dinah called them faery stories because that's what they were—stories from a faery, *her* faery. Through his deep, rumbling voice, she learned the secrets of the wood, the caches of silver and gold hidden in wooden chests and stored in riverbeds. There were teacups in the trees, silver spoons dangling from branches; someday, Orion would go there and bring back riches.

"I'll go and get what I'm owned," said the changeling. He sat at her feet and smiled up at her, goofy as ever.

"You'll leave me?" asked Dinah.

Orion shook his head. "I'll take my share, then I'll come right back. And then I'll sit on the porch and help you with the garden, and in the spring, I'll mend the fence."

"Don't go if you're goin' back for me. I don't want no riches." The sincerity in her voice shocked her. She felt the start of tears burning her eyes. "I lost one boy. I won't lose another. Orion, you gonna stay right here beside me, with us." She gestured broadly to the world, to humanity. "Maybe you weren't meant to be my child, but you're mine now. I ain't lettin' you go for nothing."

Sometimes, the changeling asked Dinah if she missed the real Orion. She told him the truth, that before, when the wound was still fresh, she thought of the boy always.

She told him that she dreamt of him dying, that there was no peace in her, not like there was nowadays.

In return, she asked him, "What happens to the children they take?"

Orion shrugged. "Maybe they grow up like I did, with new mothers."

The answer didn't satisfy Dinah. She asked, "Is there evil out there? Are there mothers? Fathers? Was there nobody to feed him? Would he survive?"

The changeling laughed. "I survived you, didn't I?"

Dinah kissed her teeth and swatted at the changeling, laughing along in spite of herself. "You wanna know what I think happens? I think he's alive, but not how I knew him. Not as a person, I mean. If he was a person, then he wouldn't be a child no more. At least, not my child. Just dirt and bones."

"And if he's not human?"

Dinah closed her eyes and brought forth the image of her boy she liked most. A magnolia tree in full bloom, the flowers fragrant. She said as much to the changeling, stroking his hair as she spoke. "In springtime, while you're mendin' the fence, he'll be in bloom. And when I'm old and tired, I'll walk into the woods and I'll sit down in his shade, and we'll be together one last time."

Orion smiled ruefully. "You think about him a lot, don't you? You love him."

"I do love him, every second of every day." Dinah sighed, cool breath blowing through the leaves, scattering petals. "But I love you too."

Years passed, and the changeling became his own man. Dinah wondered about the changeling's mother, if he'd ever go to her if she called for him, but she never entertained these thoughts for long. The changeling's place was with her, with humans. Here in her realm of people, of homes and conversation and noise, he was an oddity, but he was loved. People found him odd, but still he was found. And so, her son (for he was now, undeniably, her son) would not go back to the trees, no matter who or what called him. A changeling was loved most in retrospect, Dinah thought, when beads and bits of bark could not purchase it back.

But these were autumn thoughts, and it was spring. The magnolia tree was in bloom, and the fence needed mending.

Suddenly, I See

Midday, the afternoon splashed with warm, orange light. A familiar wends around your ankles, and the sensation of its puffed tail is all that grounds you as Agathe places three sprigs of green-white flowers onto the wooden slab that serves as your dining table. She takes a seat, and tells you to identify the poison by sight.

You are fifteen, maybe sixteen years old. Season change, time flows like a stream through the trees, but there is no age in the woods, nothing concrete. Beings are only young and agile and ripe for potions, or else they are old and foolish. The world is, for you, the sound of mad laughter, spells to turn babes into boars and men into mites. An old woman teaches you the proper way to set a curse on someone, and another shows you a potion that takes the itch out of a poison ivy rash. You know how to fly a broom, understand the basics of reading the future, and can make a sunny day wet.

You also know plants: Agathe teaches them to you. Or,

rather, Agathe presents you with bushels and sprays of green, yellow and purple, morels and mushrooms, and watches as you either choke or choose right. You were eight when you learned the difference between wild cherries and buckthorn, and ten when you nearly broke your back from spasming after ingesting nightshade. Your neck remembers how you clawed at it with uselessly blunt nails, eyes silently pleading as Agathe stared and stared. When she eventually gave you the antidote, you were suspicious of anything and everything that came from her hands. She was not insulted, your Agathe. Rather, she was proud.

Good on you, girl, for learning that no one could be trusted, not even your mother.

Not that you call Agathe "mother". There is nothing comfortable in the word, nothing that settles well in your belly. When you think of Agathe, you think of being stared through, of being lashed and scratched and punished. Also, of candies; also, of her hands petting your head gently as only she knows how.

You look over the spread of flowers, squeeze your eyes closed and open them again to clear the haze, and then you name the cuttings, left to right.

"Wild fennel, hemlock, elderflower."

You look to Agathe for confirmation, and the hag gives you nothing but a raised brow in response.

"You are certain?"

You glance at the cuttings, at Agathe's face. She betrays nothing, as always, and it is up to you to check your own work. You come closer to the table. The plants are so similar to one another, all slender green stems and sprays of white flowers. You think you might've mistaken the fennel and the elderflower, but you can't be sure. The hemlock, too, looks rather like parsnip from this angle. With a flush, you silently damn your eyes. They have, as of late, taken to crossing and blurring at odd intervals. At times, more often than not, you cannot discern one small green thing from another.

"Could I smell the plants, ma'am? To be sure?"

Cool silence coats the walls of the cabin. You avoid Agathe's eyes, though you know she is staring at you, holding you in her dark, attentive gaze.

At length, Agathe speaks, her voice like so many horseflies. "Are you a pig, Avarice?"

"Ma'am?"

"Did I transform you into a boar? Did some potion of mine grant you tusks, bristles, whiskers?" Her voices rises, rises. You back yourself up against the table. "Are you a *pig*, Avarice?"

You are unsure of how to answer, but you know that silence is a greater offense than sass. Shaking your heard, you say, "No, ma'am. I am not a pig."

"Are you certain? I only ask because as of late you have

been leaning on your nose like a leper leans on his crutch. Be it far from me to separate the common hog from her snout."

Firmer now, you say, "I am *not* a pig, ma'am."

Agathe rises to her feet and rounds the table so that she stands directly over you. In the house, she uses no illusions, no spells to hide her true form. She is wretched, hideous, all warts and pocked skin, hair tangled with twigs and grasses. Though she is hunched, she towers over you, fills the space with her rancid breath, her aura black fire smoke.

She strikes the table with her hands and says, "Tell me, then, why you insist on rooting through the plants with your nose. There is a brain in that head of yours, isn't there? Eyes? Do they not work? Come! Let *Mother* fix them."

Agathe lurches toward you, her claw-like hand poised to pluck, and you flinch away, turn your face so that she only scratches your cheek. You feel the blood bubble and flow like a tear, but you make no move to clear it. Though Agathe and the other hags have tried (and nearly succeeded) in excising all traces of fear from you, you are still afraid of what Agathe might do if she ever notices your left eye. She thrives off weaknesses, sups on the insalubrious. You are sure you'd carve out your own eyeball before giving Agathe the chance to do it for you. Better your own fingers gouging and digging than those claws, those horrible claws.

You take a breath, straighten your back. "You're right, ma'am. Might I look again?"

Agathe gestures broadly and returns to her seat. "By all means."

You turn to the table and blink your eyes once, twice, until they are in focus. Look again at the row of green and white, drawing so close that you are only centimeters away from the plants. From here, you can immediately see that you were wrong about the fennel. The narrow stems seem fuzzy, hairy like spider legs —wild carrot, certainly. You wish you could feel them, sniff at the leaves and stalks.

You say, "It is wild carrot, hemlock, and elderflower. The hemlock is in the center. Yes?"

In response, Agathe makes a curious noise. "Taste and see."

Warily, you glance at the plants. Perhaps the elder flower leaves are smaller than you first thought, the hemlock friendlier and more parsnip-like? You ask Agathe, "Is there any antidote?"

"What need you for an antidote? Now eat, girl, before I lose my patience and *do* turn you into a hog."

You nod, set the hemlock aside, and take the elderflower in hand. At first taste, you're delighted. It's green and fresh and a little sweet, like pear. You smell the cleanliness of it on your fingers and something else beneath it. Now, the wild carrot. You bring it discreetly to your nose, sniffing it from some clue. You get nothing off it, not even a whiff of soil or spring water. Now that it's between your fingers, you can no longer feel the fuzziness, the telltale bristles of a wild carrot stem. Still, Agathe is watching you, waiting for a reaction. You open your mouth and place the plant on your tongue.

Before you can chew, Agathe is giggling. Giggling and snorting, chuckling to herself like a woman gone mad. You watch her as she laughs. You know that the joke is on you, but you're not sure how. Were the plants hexed? Picked from the dung heap, leeches enchanted to look like flowers?

"What?" you say, your voice tinged with no small measure of annoyance. "What now, old woman? What evil trick have you played?"

Agathe leans back in her chair, clapping her hands and squealing with mirth. "Oh, you poor stupid girl! Better you *were* a pig and used your nose. Even a pig would know that all three sprigs were poison!" She slaps her hands together, throws back her head. "And you, smirking and chewing away at your 'elderflower'. Ha!"

Your stomach twists, your face flushes. You will not poke at the shame that comes with being wrong or the humiliation of being laughed at, but you cannot shake the callousness with which Agathe treats your life. She is all that you have, even if she has proven to you time and time again that she is not to be counted on. Though you were taught that nothing means anything, that life is naught but fleeting pleasure and the beauty of the earth, but you still expect Agathe to be kinder to you, treat you better. Had she not housed you all these years? Hadn't she prepared broths when you were ill, provided salves when you were beaten? Is she not, despite everything, your mother?

Some mother, she is. You tear through the cabin searching for antidotes and purgatives, stuffing your cheeks with marshmallow root and dandelion to the sound of Agathe's laughter. It pounds at your head, plucks at your ears. When you return to where she sits, self-satisfied and smug, you are too flustered to speak. You open and close your mouth, squeeze your eyes shut so as to block the tears, then run from the cabin.

*

Later, once you've cooled off some and the purgatives have run through the system, you return home to find Agathe perched on your bed. She holds a bundle on her lap, and lets it fall open as you near her—candied ginger and a looking glass made of silver.

"For your stomach," says Agathe, and you nod politely before sitting on your bed beside her. She pats your cheek, the cut she left there, and brings you to lay your head on her lap. You go, you let her stroke your hair like she did when you were a child. The memory of it makes you want to weep. How wicked, you think, that every bit of affection is balanced by blood.

"Poor girl," says Agathe. "Poor, foolish girl. I hope you aren't still sore with me. You'll need thicker skin than that, living in these woods."

You won't say that you had no choice in living there, won't rehash arguments on who stole whom from their father. Agathe goes on, heedless to the tears that soak her lap. "Such a sensitive thing. What shall we do with you, girl? Boil off your sweetness, pick out that candied heart of yours?" Agathe pats your cheek twice, then gently shoves you off of her. You fall back onto your pillow, blinking into the dimness of the room. "Sleep. There's a ritual tomorrow, and I don't want my prize pig asleep at the cauldron."

She leaves, closing the curtain that separates your little room from the rest of the house. When you're sure she's gone, you pop a piece of ginger into your mouth and pick up the looking glass. It's a pretty thing. You wonder what lady had it snatched off of her, what nasty spell was spoken to make her give it away. Your firstborn and a silver mirror to spin straw into gold, your little girl for a favor, a cup of sugar, a bit of rye? How much does it cost, you wonder, to owe a hag and own a child?

Late evening, a rare light in the sky and slim shadows in your room. Your candle illuminates your reflection in strange ways. You see your pocked skin, your warm skin turned sallow with sickness. You look nothing like Agathe, and yet you're everything like her, callous and cool, vicious as a viper. In some years, you'll become a great beauty, the kind of creature that lures men to their deaths and drives women mad with jealously. Something in your face will change, and you will no longer be this angry little girl, but a powerful woman, a hag born of man. Then, you think, you'll be able to pay Agathe back in kind for all that she's given you. Give her sweets, yes, but also curses and tricks, give her scratches and lashes, doses of misery and merriment in equal measure. Maybe then, when you are strong enough, you'll charm your eye straight, and be able to tell what plants have been cursed, when you've been deceived.

Until then, for now, there is only bruised skin and ego, pustules and tangled hair, and one uncentered eye, scummy and dull as a bog.

Ain't No Grave

Because of monsoon season, because there had to be a formal trial and sentencing and the mortification of the body, because Yva was damned obstinate about things being just, even if nothing else about the whole affair was just, Thomas was buried on Friday.

He would've gone down earlier, that same Tuesday even, if there'd be no one to speak for him. He knew of penitents who went into the ground just hours after being charged, the legal and holy traditions sped along and watered down to appease the masses that hungered for, above all things, fast and bloody punishment. Yva was firm, though: Thomas wouldn't be buried without a fair trial, the clergy and public opinion be damned.

It was more convenient, in the end, to change the burial date to Friday. A sinner's procession was nothing to be celebrated, but it was diverting and a good excuse to drink or eat candy apples. The gravediggers, Ezra Gelding and his cousin Gregor, stopped to buy fried bread and beer off a merchant before loading Thomas into their mule-drawn cart. Children offered the mule treats, carrots and caramels, as the clergymen read Thomas his last rites. Thomas, for his part, did nothing; clothed in nothing but rope and goose-pimpled flesh, he watched the impromptu festival from the flat of the cart, watched the stony faces of the clergy and his sister.

They left soon after, the diggers and the penitent—out of the village, through the winding paths and narrow roads of the woods, deep into the trees to where the Pits waited. The cousins chatted about the weather, the pitted roads. Thomas sat quietly and took in the deep emerald green of the woods, the rich loamy after-rain smell that rose from the ground. He liked the shape of the trees, the yew and oak. All around him was the tittering of songbirds, the autumnal breeze. Thomas added to the forest's music, humming a song he remembered from his mother, *Lālishrīta*, a lullaby. Beside him, the tools for burying—a winding sheet, the shovels, the Bible and Sacrament, the little vial of anointing oil and a bottle of wine, his casket—rolled and thumped against his legs.

By the time they reached the Pits, it was late in the afternoon. The light had changed; more golden than gray. Ezra, the smaller of the cousins, helped Thomas down off the cart and stood him by a redwood. The crush of damp leaves and berries beneath his feet was not entirely unpleasant. He let the sharp and occasional pain of stepping on twigs dull his mind, the edges of his world softening until he thought only of his discomfort and the woods that surrounded him.

Not much marked the Pits as a holy place. Repetition, maybe, the constant coming and going, the hold of tradition. Surely at some point it must've been a place of soft, pliant dirt and trees, somewhere quiet to reflect on God. There were only mounds of soil here now, some fresh and some tamped down, covered in molted, rotting leaves and mushrooms. The thicket's woven canopy made for a great, green blanket for the penitent to lie under. Sometimes, in summer, a loved one might bring by a sprig of cherry blossom or a sachet of periwinkle to adorn the land.

It wasn't consecrated ground. Everyone understood, even the youngest babe, that only the good and holy (and dead) were allowed to sleep in the church's vast graveyard. Everyone else, the wicked and evil, the sinful living, made do with the Pits.

Yva once told Thomas that the tradition was foolish, that it was a bold and callous misunderstanding of scripture to suit the wiles of men. Their father, Isai, bless his soul, had told Thomas it was something the townspeople did to feel some measure of control over their lives. The crops were unpredictable, the land temperamental; sickness and drought came at random. And, said their father, it was far easier to punish the water for spoiling than to question the dirty cup.

Of course, just weeks after he said this, Isai was buried for blasphemy. He had no trial, and his stay in the ground was short. He died almost instantly; the gravediggers had carelessly (or drunkenly) dropped him down fast. When they pulled him up two days later, his neck was bent at an ugly angle, his brown face drained of color.

All of the village agreed that it was a terrible tragedy, but unavoidable. If it were God's will, Isai would've survived the fall, would've lived the three days, and, on the third day, have risen when the trumpet called for him. Christ did, didn't He? And if Christ, God's own son, could fight his way out of the grave, push aside the stone, why couldn't any mortal? Shouldn't they all, each and every one of them, strive to be like Him?

Thomas didn't know how he felt, vis-à-vis the Pits and the theology of the ritual. Whenever he thought about the burying—all those people being swallowed up by the earth, gone for days at a time and brought back to the living by trumpet song—his mind flattened. He could think only of the relief of fresh air after being under for so long, that first horrible glare of sunlight. Unreligious, tentatively agnostic, Thomas viewed the ritual the same way he viewed everything else the village had to offer—queer, upsetting, and inexplicable.

As for his own burial, Thomas was resigned. If the villagers' God was as merciful as they claimed he was, he'd return to his sister in the allotted three days. If He wasn't, well, at least Thomas would be reunited with his father and his mother, if she was dead, as Yva thought.

Thomas wasn't so sure. He remembered little of their mother, his family having come to the village when Thomas and Yva were small children. Their mother had left not long after. There was something so hopeless about her running away. One moment she was there, warm and smelling of cardamom and allspice, and the next she was gone. Even now, grown and wiser, Thomas struggled to understand what she had been running towards. Ceylon was just a memory, more Crown than kin. Thomas couldn't fathom her running *to* the place that had spat them out. He figured she was running away from Isai and Yva and him, away from the town.

With their mother gone, Yva had been left in charge of rearing Thomas. Their father tucked his pain somewhere deep inside himself and worked, endlessly and without rest. He farmed in the warm months, did carpentry in the winter. His children waited for him at home, Yva playing mother and father both, sister and closest companion. Isai was already a ghost by the time he broke his neck. The burial was just a courtesy.

And then there were two, just Yva and Thomas against the world. Yva worked as a seamstress, and Thomas took whatever jobs he could find. The people of the village, understanding of their losses if not entirely sympathetic, lent them tools for the house, brought them food and clothes. Still, there was always that air of separation and otherness. Here they were, these strange brown foreigners from the colonies, civilized enough to wear clothes and use forks, but funny still, speaking in their odd musical language, heathenish and distant despite the thirty-odd years they'd spent in the village.

An hour passed, then two. Thomas watched the cousins Gelding grunt and heave. It was hungry work, grave digging, more punishment than honor, but honorable nevertheless. Just like him, Ezra and Gregor had committed some slight against God. Instead of being buried again (they were, both cousins, repeat offenders), the clergy put their idle hands to work rather than waste any more dirt on them.

The cousins gossiped. Thomas let their words wash over him as he twitched and swayed on his feet.

Gregor, mistaking his restlessness for impatience, chuckled. "Ah, not much longer now, Tommy-boy. Few more feet, then you can dive right in."

Ezra made a face, something between a frown and a sneer, and smacked Gregor on the back of the head. "No joking at the Pits. Ain't right, laughing at a burial."

"When you'd get to be so holy?" said Gregor as he rubbed his head. "Not like any of these poor sods can hear us, present company included." He shot Thomas a smile, his teeth shockingly yellow against his white face. "Quiet Thomas, Tongue-less Tommy—you won't tattle on us, will you?"

Thomas didn't respond. He would not quibble over his hearing nor the fact that he did, in fact, have a tongue. Better for people to think him simple, a fool, lest they pry at him. Quiet suited him fine. He spoke to his sister and those he liked in a pidgin sign language, wrote or gestured to everyone else.

He looked around, bored with the orange of Gregor's hair and captivated by the sunset. The sun was melting into the trees, daubing the brush and scrub with yellow, the greenery all bright and buttery. Above him, the gray-blue sky was cloudless. In a little more time, there'd be starlight, but by then he'd be buried. The woods were filled with all sorts of interesting sounds, sensations. There was the feather-soft touch of insects landing and scrabbling over his skin, the ants marching in strict lines over his feet. Robins and blue jays sang their final encores, their arias scored by the incessant humming of katydids.

Time moved at a snail's pace, the slime of the hours inch-inch-inching in long minutes. The cousins' chatter dulled into mere background noise as Thomas surrendered himself to the forest. He painted pictures of Yva's face against the redwood's bark with his fingernail. They were each other's mirrors, the same nose and mouth and eyes. If he died as their father did, she'd only have to grow her hair out long to see him once more.

Gregor whistled; the grave was dug and the ritual could begin. Ezra took Thomas roughly by the arm and led him to the mouth of his grave. Looking down into it was dizzying, the pitch-black soil carved deep, the sides ragged with roots and stone. From the mouth of the pit came the smell of loam and sulfur, hot and damp dirt wriggling with worms and crawling things. Thomas, momentarily planet-struck, tilted forward.

Gregor pulled him back from the edge by his rope with a grunt, then nudged him aside. Carefully, the large man unwound the burial shroud and wrapped Thomas in it, mindful to keep his face and hands free. He removed the rope from Thomas's wrists and chest, and stood aside while Ezra brought forth the sacrament, wine and oil.

They were not holy men, the cousins, but they were serious about their jobs and solemn as priests. Ezra anointed Thomas's head with the oil, letting it spill over his hair and down his forehead, onto his face and shoulders. Then, he had Thomas open his mouth so he could feed him a wine-drenched wafer. Ezra and Gregor removed the casket from the cart, opened the lid, and laid Thomas down in it.

Fear coursed through Thomas. Faced with the casket and waiting grave, he felt his mortality full force and discovered he did not want to die. Why hadn't he fought? Why hadn't he thought to bargain with the cousins? With their mercy, he might escape his fate, but Thomas knew they would not pity him.

When he was caught tumbling in the wheat with one of the farmhands, the village took it as proof of the suspicions they'd had about Thomas, his backward ways and inverted nature. These filthy people, they got up to all sorts back in their countries, didn't they? Of course, of course. The farmhand, pale and blameless (tempted, so said the clergy, by dark magic), disappeared, and Thomas was rounded up, shamed. He imagined, had the boy been punished, it wouldn't have been nearly as brutal as his comeuppance, so there was no good in it. Anyways, Thomas was confused with the rules regarding sex. Just a few weeks ago, Michael Keene was found with his hand up Molly's skirt and the next day was seen running from Annette's bedroom bare as he was born. The most he got was a tongue-wagging, a few raised eyebrows. Why then, Thomas wondered, was he paraded around town with such vile words around his neck, mocked and scorned, beaten and bloodied? What separated their sins?

And, Thomas thought, was it really such a sin? The Bible, that thing of onion-paper and leather, was just bursting with begats and begots. Hadn't David loved Jonathan? Judas kissed the Savior's ear, and Peter loved Jesus so dearly, so purely. When Thomas brought the farmhand into the field with him, he wanted only to hold the man and be held, slip wheat between the charming gap in his teeth, and smell the warm freshness of his skin mingled with the hay. He couldn't see the evil in their loving, even if it was temporary.

There was no saying such things to the cousins. Too much separated them and not enough bound them. Maybe if Thomas was paler, more talkative. Maybe if Yva wasn't so pretty and reserved, holding her chin up in the town square even as others cowered. Maybe if Isai wasn't brown and gruff, if their mother hadn't run from the village just months after arriving...

If only, if only, but ifs served for little. Thomas flexed his hands and twisted at the limited range of motion the winding sheet gave him. He bade his heart to still itself as the casket's lid was brought down on him with a definitive thump. Thomas pressed his hands to the wood—it would not give, not even a millimeter. It'd be very hard to get out of, once he was underground.

One of the cousins said, "Shall you say the words, or me?"

The other said, "I'll do it."

Thomas imagined them bowing their heads and closing their eyes, hands clasped together in prayer. The chosen cousin, Ezra most likely, said, "Dear Lord, we bring unto you a wretched soul. It is flawed and it is wicked. Only you can redeem it. Just as you saw fit to bury and raise your own son, we ask you to do the same to Thomas. Let him die in flesh, let him rise in spirit. Reawaken his dry bones. We return him, this vile thing, to the earth from which it came..."

From whence *it came*, corrected Thomas. He signed out the rest of the prayer as best he could, following along with Ezra's stilted, uncertain reading. *From dirt we came, made of your spit, and to dirt we return. Your will be done, make him anew.*

"Amen," said the cousins.

"Amen," signed Thomas.

They moved him slowly. Sightless, cut off from the world, Thomas tried to picture the stars, the look of the trees over the cousins' heads as they lowered him down. His chest tightened; he was going under, under. A slip of the hands and he'd fall, break his neck. He listened as dirt and stone scraped the sides of the casket, the earth eating him foot by foot. He listened, heart in his throat, to the sound of his blood loudening, rushing, his stomach twisting and spoiling. There was bile on his tongue, bitter wine and wafer, and he swallowed it down. The anointing oil made the shroud cling to his skin. He couldn't breathe, he couldn't *breathe*. He wanted to peel off his skin like a coat, let it sit beside him as he made sense of the darkness, the complete silence of being under the earth.

Now, Thomas was in it. Under it. Through the wood of the casket, he smelled hot soil and oil, his terrified sweat. He wouldn't scream, not yet. He held himself perfectly still while soil rained down on the casket shovelful after shovelful. After a while, there was no more shoveling and no more sound. Thomas heard nothing, felt nothing.

The earth swallowed him whole, and Thomas fell down, down, down into its belly.

*

On that first day, Thomas screamed. Stupid waste of time and breath, foolish, but he was only human, and afraid. When he woke from restless sleep, he had no way of telling the time. He only knew that it was dark and too hot, quiet and close and suffocating. He drew in a breath, realized there wasn't much air to be had, then started wailing. Like a babe or a madman, he shrieked and cried, clawed at the wood of his casket until his fingernails tore off, fought and twisted his winding sheet until it was down around his ankles. Single-minded, Thomas slammed his head against

128

the wood until his forehead was wet, blood pouring like holy oil down into his eyes. Another anointing, a crown of splinters in his hair. When he finally grew dizzy with exhaustion, he threw himself onto his back, keened and whined piteously like a kicked dog.

Come the second day, Thomas again fought his bonds. In between fits of anger and bursts of frantic kicking and screaming, he thought of his sister. Poor Yva, he thought, slamming his hands against the roof of the casket. Poor Yva, abandoned to live amongst people who disdained her, damned to never again hear someone speak to her in Tamil. Thomas saw her face, her tired brown eyes and worried mouth. What would she do without him? The loneliness of being the only person who looked like she did would gut her, and a mirror would provide little relief. Yva needed someone to drink chai with, someone who knew their mother's tongue, someone to brush and braid her hair, to ask for stories of Ceylon. Someone had to be there to sing *Lālishrīta* in their mother's warbling voice.

It was not that Thomas doubted his sister's competency. There were few women in the village as hardy or hardworking as she. It was only the strength of her heart he doubted, how much grief she could hold before her arms finally gave out.

His face was wet, with blood or with tears. Thomas rubbed his cheeks roughly, took a deep breath, and rested both hands on the casket's ceiling. *Now,* thought Thomas. *Now, it's time to rise.*

*

On the third day of Thomas's punishment, the sky cracked open. Yva didn't know what scared her more, the gray wall of rain or the cracks of lightning. She thought of her mother, her stories of Indra and his mighty thunderbolt, Vajra. She thought of Thomas underground, his freedom hampered by mud.

Four days after Thomas had been buried, Yva packed a little lunch, filled a canteen with water, and walked to the Pits. The clergy was of no use to her. Thrice, she'd gone before them and begged for mercy, for Thomas's body to be returned to her so she could prepare it for a proper burial. Thrice, she'd been denied. Armed now with nothing but love, Yva went where she was forbidden to go. She rode no white elephant, carried no quiver full of lightning; she relied only on her two weary feet to carry her the countless miles to the Pits. She sang as she walked, little things she remembered from her parents. She spoke to herself, to Thomas, and tried to view the world through his eyes. He would've loved the dull gray of the sky, the stretch of the trees. She imagined her brother walking by her side, his atonal humming a pleasant companion. Here and there, he stopped to pick up colorful stones, or nudged Yva's side to point out brightly colored birds, funny-looking insects.

When she arrived at the Pits, she was dismayed to find her imagination was not far off. Rain made the ground slick and muddy. Trees lay felled over mounds of dirt, heavy branches blocking whole swaths of the ground. Yva's stomach flipped as she walked through the debris—her brother was here beneath her feet, mud and timber separating them.

What a wicked place! These people dared to call *her* a heathen, a pagan! Well, *her* kind never thought to bury people alive for the sake of redemption, never even imagined sealing a living thing away to appease a cold, jealous god. There was something so malignant about it all, the symbols and crosses, the single-minded focus on sin and mortification, the wickedness of the flesh.

The body was not an evil thing. Yva remembered their mother stressing to her the goodness of her hands, the strength of her feet. Beautiful brown skin, beautiful deep eyes; certainly, her mouth could get her into trouble, and her mind might think unkind things, but always at the core of her, at the bottom of her soul, she was good. There was nothing wicked about the curve of her mouth, nothing unholy about Thomas's silence. That the village would send him to his death for putting his body to use was unthinkable to her. Looking over the wreckage of the Pits,

131

she wished she'd fought harder to keep him above ground.

As she walked and took in the storm's damage, Yva came across a sunken patch of land. The sides were jagged, and she looked into the deep mouth of it. It smelled of loam and sulfur, the hot green breath of the earth. She strained her eyes. Was that... There, just there, was that the lid of a casket? Her heart leapt into her throat.

She fell to her knees, planted them firmly in the dirt. Yes, there was the empty casket. Yva saw the dingy white of the winding sheet, splashed and speckled with blood. Each shift of the wind brought up another belch of hot, rank air—bodily waste, mud, and man combined. There were half-moon-shaped fingernails embedded into the dirt. Leaning over as far she could without tumbling down into the grave, Yva pried two of the fingernails out of the soil as proof of him having been there, though what she meant to prove and to whom she wasn't quite sure.

Slowly now, Yva rose to her feet. She looked around herself, hands cupping her elbows. Sunlight filtered in through the canopy, green and yellow. Birdsong rang out, undercut by the buzzing of crickets, katydids. She considered her jagged breath and the loneliness of the village that awaited her. She considered her father's grave, the empty space where her mother once stood. Off in the distance, buried beneath the whine of insects, a bubbling far-off brook, there was another sound. She strained her ears to listen. Yes, it was like something humming, atonal and off-key; *Lālishrīta,* their mother's lullaby.

Something Got a Hold of Me

There weren't many people that visited the first lady's office at the Blessed Streams Missionary Baptist Church. It was private, a little side-room branching off from the church's main office, more courtesy than clerical. Something about its positioning made people wary of it. It was a woman's space, decidedly feminine, tucked between the nursery and the women's restroom. The whole of the hallway was tainted by it, the perfumed air, how the walls almost rippled with a sort of sanctified sensuality, mysterious, but altogether very proper.

Just three other women had been first lady before Comfort Williams took up the post. Their portraits lined the wall of the "women's hall" that led into the office, a skirt-suited preview of what was to come. First was Sister Marsha Collins, the church founder's wife, demure in her pearls and elaborate white hat; then there was sister Irene Holding, her nervous eyes and embarrassed, toothless smile; and then, Sister Gladys Suns, beaming brightly out of her frame, effervescent even in front of that drab, gray marbled background.

And then, finally, almost as an afterthought, there was herself, Sister Comfort Williams, serene and reserved, a string of pearls around her neck. She smiled softly, careful not to show many teeth. It was tacky, thought Comfort, to be seen baring your teeth like an ape.

It wasn't easy, being the new first lady. Comfort constantly battled nostalgia, sentimental brothers and sisters who remembered times way back when. Sister Collins said, and Sister Holding had, and Sister Suns would never. Every day was an uphill battle as she tried to contort herself into whatever the congregation at Blessed Streams wanted. Quieter, neater, more reserved, more modest, more and more, less and less.

She couldn't share her troubles with nobody. The one person she could've told was her husband, but he was pastor at Blessed Streams and everything came easy to him. He'd been sworn in some months after Pastor Suns's passing, and the church took him in without so much as a blink. All he had to do was show up on time, preach the Word, don't say nothing too new or exciting, shout a little, and rouse a little holy excitement. At the end of the day, he'd get his plate from the fellowship hall, the biggest piece of chicken for the preacher.

And what did Comfort get? Chicken? Handshakes? Oh,

no, *no*, never. She got the silent treatment, cold shoulders and colder looks, sidelong glances at the length of her skirt, the red of her nails. Her children were too messy, her husband's clothes not quite pressed enough. Boy-children with scruffy hair were proof of a disordered home. A girl-child who even so much as shifted in her pew, perhaps to relieve some of the ache from sitting on hard wood, was cause for stern talking-tos. Don't you have any control over your home? Why are your children so free? And if she, Comfort, ever dared to look bored, to yawn, to be less than starched and glimmering every day of the week but especially on Sunday, why then, Comfort didn't even want to imagine the sort of chaos that'd inspire.

She wasn't her own thing, not any more. She was the Church, and the Church was with her, and the Church *was* her, and if she wanted to stay at Blessed Streams, Lord knew, she had best act like it.

Eventually, though, Comfort got it. After five years of pushing and pulling, of bullying and being bullied, of being called in and talked to, of being pinched and shaded and lectured, she was, more or less, accepted by the congregation. There were certain powers and privileges she had, she learned. For example, no one could question the first lady wresting control from the deaconesses and pastor's aides, same as they couldn't quibble when she took control over the sewing ministry and prayer breakfasts.

Powerless in all other places, she took what she could. She'd won.

But now, *this*. This being, of course, that ugly thing that happened at the last revival service. Comfort shuddered to think of it again, how quickly it came upon them all and how long it went on, the dead silence that followed in the aftermath.

It'd been late, the sanctuary hot despite the season. At three weeks deep, the winter revival was at its peak, Spirit ripping through the church like a storm, churning people up, making the blood run hot with holiness. The air was sludge-thick with perfume and cologne, body funk and sweat and baby powder. Harlan, the organ player, pounded furiously at the keys, the drums and tambourines struggling to keep up with him. Then there was the clapping, the stomping, the swaying—everything in motion, everything writhing.

Comfort had been sat in the front row. She clapped and swayed along, interested in the music but alert. She glanced around. There were babies fast asleep, heads propped up by whatever purse was nearest. Mothers cooled themselves with hand fans and programs. People were started to be taken in by it, the music and the movement. There went Sister Jerricka, hair coming out of her bun and falling messily into her face. There, just a pew or so back from Jerricka, was Sister Liz, modesty panel loosed by the force of her dancing. And over there, Brother Zach, full up of Jesus, eyes rolling to the back of his head.

All around her, folks were screaming, whooping, carrying on. Comfort kept herself still; she liked the theatrics of a holy rapture, the way it struck like lightning and set a whole sanctuary ablaze, but had to stay out of it herself. There wasn't any dignity in it, and anyways, she had a reputation to uphold.

When the shrieking began, Comfort wasn't sure what to make of it. It wasn't like any praise *she'd* ever heard. It was bloodcurdling, sharp enough to pierce through the music. Nobody else seemed to hear it or pay it any mind, at first. They thought that the Spirit was taking somebody over, God doing somersaults in their heart and belly. It was a bit much for Comfort, the screaming, and she hoped it'd be over soon, but the shrieking went on and on, through the music, through that first lurch of organ keys that invited dancing and stepped down the aisles, all through the spasming and whooping and speaking in tongues, and even long after everyone else had cooled down.

That high voice cut through the quiet of prayer, screaming, "The blood! The blood! The blood!"

Comfort turned in her seat to see who was making all that ruckus and grimaced. Of course, it was *her*. Ursula Dupree was a tall and meatless woman, gangly and strange, all elbows and knees in her wrist-to-ankle dress. She screamed, on and on, the veins in her neck and forehead straining like worms beneath her skin. One of the nurses padded down the aisle quietly, quickly, a box of tissues in one hand and a comfort shawl draped over her arm. Three ushers followed her, toothy men with broad and careful smiles, ready to assist.

It should've been handled calmy. It should've been over within seconds, but then the girl reared back, spine bending into a terrible arch, whole body forming a "c", then brought her head forward and down—*crack!*—hard on the pew in front of her. That first connection shot through the church like crunching wood. Comfort could almost see the knot forming, the streak of blood pooling over the girl's left eye. People watched in horror as Ursula again and again threw back her body and slammed her face into the unyielding wooden pew. Blood poured down her face like water, like anointing oil. It dripped down into her eyes, over her streaming nose and mouth, and still, she did not stop.

The nurse reached for her, panicking now, but Ursula avoided her hands. Blinded by red, she stumbled into the aisle, hands outstretched in front of her, and fell, face-first, onto the carpet. She rolled over onto her back, the movement as sensuous and skittering as the death spasms of a roach. She clawed at herself, dragging her nails down the flesh of her arms, her legs, clawed at her neck and collarbone. She rolled her eyes, bloodshot and bloody, until there was nothing to see there but white. All the while, she cried out, "The blood! The blood!"

Comfort could not say what she felt, watching the girl. Horror? Disgust? She was naught but a piteous thing writhing there on the electric-blue carpet. The sight of her, pressed hair sweating out, falling down into her face, fingers leaving welts on her light skin—it was all too much. Ursula gouged the palms of her hands until they bled, then dug at her side with jagged, bitten-down nails until that ran with blood as well.

Comfort tore her eyes away, shook away the shock, and gave her husband a quick, pressing look. His brows were furrowed, seemingly more annoyed at his service being interrupted than affected by the show the girl was putting on. Silently, the couple questioned one another. What should we do? Do we remove her? Reverend Williams nodded. Comfort waved over two of the stronger deacons and a handful of ushers and told them, quietly, to remove Ursula from the sanctuary.

This too was a struggle. Even after the men had managed to cover Ursula in the comfort shawl, she fought. Her nails and teeth were inescapable, and many of the men came away with scrapes, bites. Still, she was hefted, kicking and spasming, out of the sanctuary through one of the discreet exits.

Later in the nurse's station, Ursula lay on a crisp white

sheet. She was washed in scarlet, bruised and gashed. Her eyes were glazed over, unfocused. Comfort stood beside the cot, arms crossed over her chest, as the nurse poked at the girl, lifted her eyelids, and asked questions. Ursula did nothing, said nothing. Now that she was out of the sanctuary (away from an audience, thought Comfort coolly), the girl was quiet, trembling on the cot, lurching now and again to spit up wine-colored bile into the nearby wastebasket.

An ambulance arrived. One of the deacons tagged along to keep her company. More out of obligation than any real feeling, Comfort patted Ursula's hand and make a weak promise to come and see her in the hospital, knowing as she said it that she had no intention of going to visit the girl. It was disquieting enough to sit in the nurse's station with her—she cringed to think of herself alone with the girl in a hospital room, strangers looking in on them, expecting her to have some encouraging words to say to this *thing*.

As the days passed and the echoes of Ursula's screams faded, Comfort excused herself time and time again. Something came up, plans changed. She let her husband, Rufus, go in her stead, and when he returned, Comfort listened with disinterest as he recounted the visit. Each time he returned from Ursula's bedside, his face was wan and drawn, closed. When she asked after the girl—prodding lightly, curious only in the way a child is curious about the actions of an earthworm—Rufus would rub at his mouth and shake his head before drifting off to his study, his silence confirming all sorts of nasty truths.

Now, there was no more avoiding Ursula. After two months in the hospital and another two weeks recuperating at home, it was decided (by others, not by *her*) that Ursula should talk to Sister Comfort. Some busybody from the women's ministry suggested it—Ursula was young, she'd just been through something horrifying, and she needed guidance, didn't she, from an older woman.

"You can steer her right," said the lady. She had a smirking, patronizing quality to her that made Comfort want to smack her right in the face, but Comfort only smiled, nodded. "Ain't nobody in the whole church can help her but you, Sister."

Woman to woman, they said—sister to sister. Comfort was pressed and urged, wheedled and guilted. Wasn't this one of her main duties? If she couldn't stop this sort of thing from happening, the gore and ruined pew, then how could she be trusted to handle the smaller things?

Comfort knew they were right, but she still didn't want to do it. She didn't want the girl in her office. She was unnerving, upsetting. Something about the way Ursula held herself, her funny way of walking and talking which extended way past her little performance in the sanctuary. It couldn't be rationalized. Comfort, a woman who lived in the black-and-white, who liked life clear and simple and clean-cut, could not abide with things such as Ursula; queer and askew, as impossible to know as God's own mind.

Her office was her safe space. It was just as she liked it—air-conditioned, carpeted, outfitted with all matter of small comforts. A photograph of her with her children—the epitome of Christian womanhood, Comfort seated with her two broad-shouldered boys behind her, and her gently smiling daughter standing just a little ahead of her—hung over above a pink, button-tufted armchair. Across from it sat another chair, a tall wicker structure with a cushion she had sewn herself. On the walls were a dozen or so hoops embroidered with Bible verses. There were paintings, of course—a child being spoon-fed pages from the Bible; a dark and smiling Jesus looking fondly over lambs and woolly-haired children; a quartet of round-hipped Black women clasping hands and raising their long necks in song. Comfort kept all the cards sent to her in plain view and the letters tucked away in a desk drawer. Drawings made by the youngest of the youth group were tacked to her bulletin board, along with flyers for the upcoming church jumble sale and the canned-food drive. All the books on her white bookshelf were on homemaking, clean living, and bringing up holy households. On an end table sat doilies and bowls of hard candies, a vase of false flowers.

It was only natural that Comfort felt so undone by the

thought of Ursula coming into her space. The girl simply did not belong. But she was coming, and Comfort sat in her wicker chair, folded her hands in her lap, and waited for her arrival. She darted her eyes to the wall clock. It was a quarter after three; Ursula was late. Comfort drummed her nails on the chair's arm.

Twenty minutes later, there was a soft knock at the door. Comfort leapt to her feet and opened it, fixing her face into her trademark, toothless smile. Standing at the threshold was Ursula, face green-yellow with bruises. There was a garish pink scar on her forehead, about two inches in length, and a smaller scar above her right eye. Her gaze was unfocused, and she came through the door stiffly, arms straight at her side. She was aware enough to find her way to the pink armchair without assistance, much to Comfort's relief.

Comfort looked the girl over as she sat. Ursula was dressed head to toe in dark garments, everything from her neck down to her knees obscured by a black woolen dress. Thick black tights covered the rest of her legs, and on her feet were big, blocky shoes. Only her hands were visible, and even those were obscured by the wads of white gauze wrapped around her palms.

Clearing her throat, Comfort took her seat across from Ursula. "So, Sister Ursula... how have you been?"

Nearly too quietly to hear, Ursula responded that she

was fine.

A beat of awkward silence followed, and Comfort rushed to fill it. "Good, good. Home's okay? I know they had you in the hospital for a good while."

Ursula lifted her head a little. "You said you'd visit me, and you never did."

Comfort flushed. "Yes, well, I *am* sorry for that. I got busy, but I still should've set aside time for you." She put a hand to her chest and said, "Charge it to my head and not my heart, sister. I'm sorry."

Again, silence overtook the room. The stop-start nature of their conversation was already beginning to grate on Comfort. She rubbed her hands on her knees and cleared her throat again.

Ursula looked down at her lap. Comfort saw very little of her now—only her oily scalp was visible, the sharp middle part of her hair. Her stockinged knees were akimbo, and Comfort cringed at the look of her, broken and unseemly in the fine, plush chair, confused at her own being there.

Straining for civility, Comfort said, "Sister Ursula, I'm sure you know why you've been asked to come to see me. I'm sorry, again, I didn't get to do this earlier, in the hospital, but better late than never, hm?" She smiled tightly, saw that Ursula wouldn't see it, and dropped it. "To be frank, sister, I'm worried about you. Do you remember any of what happened to you? That Wednesday?"

"Got the Holy Spirit," Ursula mumbled.

Comfort let out a puff of air through her nose. "Yes, well, maybe it was, and maybe it wasn't. It's all very easy, you see, to *claim* it was the Holy Spirit coming over us, but let's consider that it wasn't, for a second. Did the doctors say anything to you? A stroke or an aneurysm, something like that?"

Ursula shook her head slowly, her flat-pressed hair waving like a greased flag of defeat. "No stroke, ma'am. No medicine." She strained her shoulders forward and sighed out long and slow. "*Spirit.*"

Comfort inhaled deeply, fighting tooth and nail against the annoyance building in her chest. In all other circumstances, with anyone else, she'd be all for the suggestion of the Holy Spirit. She was brought up in churches like Blessed Streams, whooping and hollering places that encouraged letting God take over the body. If she weren't ordained to be silent and serene, she'd be the sort of woman who kicked off her shoes and went stepping down the aisles, the type to lash her body and scream for glory. Once, when she was a girl, Comfort watched a woman at her mother's home church fall to her knees and crawl around like a baby, singing the psalms. That level of holy passion excited her, and Comfort sneered to think that somebody like Ursula should ever be allowed to feel it.

She wasn't shy to admit that she was stingy about God. He was not meek, nor was He mild. *Her* God drowned sinners, struck down harlots, punished and tested even his most loyal of servants with boils, great whales, and other such tribulations. Her God didn't associate with people like Ursula, with sinners, with oddballs, with people who just wouldn't adjust. Core tenets of the religion be damned, Comfort could not hold with dirt and dirties, with poverty, with untended children and the squalor of the desperate. Comfort's own family was just one generation out of poverty, but she *was* better now, better than them dirty people, better than Ursula. She was saved by the Blood, washed white and clean, superior to those great sins of untidiness, of slovenliness, and worse of all, an empty purse.

She might be more receptive to the girl, Comfort wondered, if Ursula was pretty. If Ursula weren't so bony and quiet, if she weren't so tall, if she were proud but not prideful, if her voice was sweet and not whispering, and if she laughed more often, or maybe just smiled, Comfort could let herself be a little kinder to the young sister. If she sang, maybe, or participated in any of the ministries available to young women, and maybe if she weren't so prone to staring dumbly down at her threadbare little Bible, all marked-up and old, with little care for the fellowship aspect of the church. But alas, Ursula was as she was and not at all the way Comfort wanted her to be. She just wasn't good enough, unworthy of the Spirit and of Comfort's God.

"Okay, then," said Comfort, calmly as she knew how. "Let's say then that you *were* under the Spirit. You still gave everyone an awful scare, what with your little performance."

"It had me, under the veil."

"The veil?"

"The *shawl*." Ursula lifted her head and furrowed her dark brows. "It was over my face, over all of me."

Comfort exhaled, exasperated. She waved her hand and said, "Oh, child, everybody goes under the shawl if they catch the Spirit. That still doesn't explain why you were acting the way you were. You were *hurting* yourself, Sister Ursula. Slamming your head into the pew. It was starting to scare the other members."

"No need to fear," breathed Ursula. "Was only…" She inhaled sharply through her mouth and hissed it out through her nose. She seemed to struggle with her words, wrestling them down. In the end, Ursula won out and said, "My tongue weren't my tongue. My hands weren't my hands. His hands, ma'am. *His* tongue."

"His tongue?" Comfort pulled herself even further away from Ursula. She felt herself making a face, but couldn't quite will it away. "Sister Ursula, if this was some sort of *sexual* thing…"

"Sexual? No, not sexual, Sister Comfort. Not at all. It was..." Ursula eased herself all the way back into the chair and stretched out her legs, long and taut enough to snap. "I heard the choir singing, the organ, and everything felt so close. Like Mr. Harlan was playing right in my heart, and the tambourine ladies were shaking my bones, and the drums... The drums, *bump*, *bump*, *tss-tss-tss*, all through me, even behind my eyes, and then I didn't feel it at all. I was then I wasn't. Something got a hold on me. I was on fire. Itching, *itching*, burning." Ursula widened her eyes. "You ever been burned before, Sister Comfort?"

Comfort shook her head, wary. "No. Cooking burns, sometimes."

"T'ain't like nothing you think you can survive, sister. Felt like I was drenched in oil, like somebody washed me down in holy oil and set me ablaze. But there weren't no smoke, Sister Comfort; just pain. Just my body screaming out and fighting and itching, and when I looked down at myself, I see me, covered in blood." Ursula grimaced, shook her head and squeezed her eyes shut. "I *felt* it, sister. Thick and syrupy, like molasses, oozing slow and slow, purple-black over me. It was coming from my hands, from my side. I was scared, so scared, but I was at peace too, because the blood was keeping me cool, even while I was burning sum'n awful. I could hear me screaming and felt my body twisting, winding up, but it wasn't really my body no more.

Just a vessel. Just an empty thing for *Him*."

"Him?"

"Christ, Sister Comfort." The name came from her mouth like wind. "His blood was my blood, and I saw myself upon the cross, beaten and pierced, and I saw myself like I really was too, all beaten up and hurting myself. I'd been baptized before, Sister Comfort. Dipped in a river when I was a just a li'l girl." Her voice dipped low and it shook, too excited and nervous to lie still. "I was beneath the water, and I felt the same way that Wednesday, like I was drowning in it, the fire and the Lamb's blood. It was all in my throat, in my veins. Jesus was in *me*."

As Ursula spoke, she stretched her neck and pushed herself out long, straining so far that the veins in her neck and legs were like steel wires. She gripped onto the chair's arms, her blunted fingernails scraping against the pink.

"Transcended," whispered Ursula. "I had transcended." She blinked her eyes open. "He took me over, Sister Comfort. I weren't even there."

Silence, stillness. All throughout Ursula's story, Comfort's mind was working double-triple time to make sense of what she was hearing. What Ursula describe was the familiar testimony of religious rapture. That delicious, all-consuming sensation of Him, of the Trinity suddenly filling a body to the brim.

This orgasmic love of Christ, it wasn't Ursula's to have.

Comfort seethed. What did that girl have that she didn't? What part of Comfort, clean and tidy, repelled God while Ursula twisted and spasmed with the full weight of Him? Comfort took in a sharp breath and turned her face to the side so Ursula wouldn't see the extent of her rage, the blue-hot heat that was bubbling up from her belly and burning her face.

Ignorant to Comfort's ire, Ursula relaxed into the armchair. Her limbs loosened, and she wore a look of dazed contentment. She took long, deep breaths, gently touched a hand to her heart.

Composing herself, Comfort said, "Sister Ursula, while I can't claim to know what was happening in your mind, I can say I think you're telling a fib. I think you liked the attention your show gave you, everybody turning their eyes to look at you. I think you're unkempt; I think you're slovenly and slothful. Look at you, sister. You are in the house of the Lord! You come here, week after week after week, dressed in rags, joyless in the presence of He who gives joy to all. You should be ashamed of yourself, Ursula. Shamed and afraid for your soul, coming in here, spinning stories on God Himself."

"Ain't no lie!" In a burst of movement, Ursula pushed herself up straight and met Comfort's gaze with her own. Facing her head-on was alarming—her eyes blazed. "You think I'd hurt myself like this? Beat myself bloody? For what?"

"Attention, notoriety..." Comfort crossed and uncrossed her arms. Looked at Ursula and then quickly away. "I don't know your mind, girl."

"You couldn't! What would you know?" The girl jerked forward in her chair, body trembling. All of her previous calm had dissipated and been replaced by tight, snapping anger that seemed just barely under control. "You rather think I'd bash my head in for attention than believe somebody like *me*, somebody unclean and plain..." Ursula interrupted her speech with a frustrated growl. "Somebody *ungodly* and unnatural, could be taken by Him, chosen by Him, changed and seen and loved simply because you wouldn't choose me. Well, Sister *Williams*, He did choose me. Out of all of them saints, over *you*, He picked me." At that, Ursula rose to her feet, smoothed down her dress, and walked towards the door. She opened it, stopped, and looked back at Comfort, who sat, flinching, in her chair. Softly, Ursula said: "Maybe you don't know God as well as you thought, sister, if mine eyes have seen the glory, and yours have seen nothing but wickedness."

She left, closing the door after her. Alone again in her office, alone with her trappings and comfort, her small pleasures, Comfort panted through her nose. She looked around herself—her chairs, her cards, the cherubs gazing beatifically at their winged and harped teachers. Her Bible sat on the desk, heavily engraved but mostly untouched. Comfort's hands twitched in her lap, little flicking motions.

Her eyes drew to her framed picture of Christ. He was open-handed and doe-eyed. Comfort stared at him, the brown paint strokes of His hair and the silky texture of His robe, tied with a humble rope. She looked to Jesus—looked *through* Jesus—and her Lord and Savior looked right back.

A Girl Walks Alone

Elsie never feared walking alone, not before. People didn't scare her, and she was always in good company when by herself. She liked feeling in community with the world around her, the people and places that made a city home. What did she have to worry about when she knew the men who sat in front of the corner store like uncles; the unhoused folks and vagrant teens like siblings, cousins?

The world felt built for her, crafted especially for her joy and pleasure, and even if such imaginings were naught but a young woman's folly, they were real enough for Elsie.

Even at night, when she had everything and everyone to fear, Elsie was unafraid. There was peril, there was danger, but there were also gorgeous flashing lights, neon and electric, and music spilling out from every bar and nightclub on the strip. From this scrubby place, twangy honky-tonk music coasted on plumes of cigarette smoke. From that hookah spot, the smell of hash and herbs thumping alongside trap music, neo-soul, some vibey hip-hop better suited for smoking than dancing. And the people! This glorious, cacophonous mess of humanity assembled! What a piece of work was mankind, what perfect design! Here they were dancing, grinding, flirting, arguing, kissing, fighting, play-fighting, smoking, drinking, laugh-and-laugh-and-laughing. *Yes*, thought Elsie. Yes, this is loud and messy and too much, but I love it. She closed her eyes, let the din of the night wash her over, and fell happily into the noise.

It had been a good night out. One of Elsie's girlfriends had gotten a promotion, and they celebrated by spending the evening hopping from bar to restaurant (Korean barbecue, Elsie's treat) to a little ice cream place, and then, finally a trendy nightclub the women had dubbed their "spot". Yvonne, the lady of the hour, was fall-over drunk, giddy and dizzy and physically supported by Erika, the night's designed driver and killjoy.

Yvonne stood outside of the nightclub, chanting, "One more bar! One more bar!" Erika and Elsie shared fond, exasperated looks.

"Absolutely *not*. Nuh-uh, no way. Your ass is way too lit to be going anywhere but to bed," said Erika. She unfolded Yvonne's coat from over her arm while Elsie tugged down Yvonne's dress, which was inching its way up her legs.

"But it's *so-o* early! Elsie, tell her! Tell her it's too early to be going home!"

Elsie threw up her hands in mock surrender. "Girl, don't look at me. It is two in the goddamn morning."

Yvonne pouted, crossed her arms, accused Erika and Elsie of being lame and fake, but in the end, Erika managed to wrangle Yvonne into her car. As Yvonne struggled to buckle herself in, Erika let Elsie know she'd be taking Yvonne back to her own place.

"She don't never wanna go nowhere, but when you get her out..." Both women looked over at Yvonne, already half-sleep, head bobbing against the headrest. "Chile, let me get this girl to bed 'fore she hurt herself."

Erika slipped into the car, rolled down the windows. "Get home safe, okay? Text me as soon as you get in."

Elsie nodded, warm and sleepy. Yvonne leaned over Erika and yelled out the window, "Be safe, Elsie! Be safe!"

As the car pulled away from the curb, Elsie wondered why her friends worried so much. She was a big girl, svelte but tall and formidable. Anyways, nothing could hurt her. In her party dress, in her heels, she was invincible. The world was cradling her; she felt its heartbeat in every car bumping its bass, the click-clack of her shoes.

Elsie walked home. Another benefit of living in the heart of the city; her apartment was just around the corner from the nightlife. She'd hear Ari Lennox until the wee hours of the morning, her dreams tinted blue with R&B groove.

She walked, she watched. Some drunk dude called out to

her, and Elsie ignored him, her shoulders drawn into herself until she was certain he wouldn't try to follow her. She'd been followed before, once. She knew what it was like to have a shadow, calling after you like a lost cat. *Here, kitty-kitty. Here, long legs, red dress! Yeah, mama, I see you!* Elsie held onto her house keys, mapped out the terrain of her purse; her Taser, pocket knife and mace, all pink and glittery and dangerous.

The night deepened; music from the clubs faded to a dull roar and the street lamps buzzed to life. Elsie clicked past the rows and rows of apartments, condos. She hummed the chorus of a song she'd heard at the club. Her dress, purple and blue and gaudily sequined, sparkled attractively under the orange glow of the street lamps.

Then she felt it. That tingle of fear, that itch of being watched. Anxiety, icy and wet, dripped down her spine, made a pool of sweat at the small of her back. She drew herself in, folded in her shoulders. Elsie heard herself breathing fast, far off music, cars. Suddenly, she was hyper-conscious of her dress, the danger of it. She felt like a spectacle, a beacon, something bright and terrible inviting unfriendly gazes.

Elsie waited a beat, gathered her courage, gathered her keys between her knuckles, turned, and—

Nothing.

There was nothing behind her, no one trailing her, no

entitled asshole casing the joint. The night was dark but illuminated, and all Elsie saw was shrubbery and litter.

She laughed nervously. *Silly*, she thought. She was being silly, freaking herself out and making stalkers out of street signs. Elsie shook it off, squared her shoulders and walked (a little more urgently) to her apartment.

The elevator that took her up to her apartment always smelled like piss and weed, but at least it was faster than the stairs. Elsie loosened her grip and her posture. She thought of home, thought of her bed, her room decorated with her little curios.

Close now, only a long, dim hallway away. The lights were temperamental on this floor, more off than on. Elsie made a mental note to complain to the super, even though he rarely fixed things.

Click, click, click down the hallway, lights flickering above her head. Elsie muttered to herself about high rent and low living. She had reached her door when the feeling of being watched came back in full force. *Now*, Elsie thought. *Now there's something really there, something too damn close.* She listened to the quiet and past the quiet. She heard the neighbor's TV blaring, someone upstairs stomping, someone downstairs arguing. The hall lights flickered and buzzed.

Elsie stilled her hands enough to unlock the door. Put her hand on the knob.

A breath. A single puffed breath was her only warning before it was on her. Elsie grunted as she was thrown to the floor in a rush of movement, darkness. Fabric whipped wildly; a flag caught in a gust of wind. The thing hissed a terrible scratchy cat's hiss, loud in Elsie's ear. Confused, panicky, Elsie grabbed for her purse, for her pastel instruments of protection, but the creature pinned her down, trapping her beneath its massive weight.

Locked between the brown carpet and the creature, Elsie saw her attacker in its totality. It was revolting, repulsive— half-human, half-beast, all glowing red eyes and a mouth comprised of snarling lips and razor-sharp teeth. It smelled foul, like death and blood and rot, body funk and musk.

Faint with nausea, prone and stiff with shock, Elsie stared up at the creature. She didn't dare struggle or scream, and she wasn't sure her body would let her anyway, had she had the will or wherewithal to do so. She whimpered as the thing brought its flat, bat-like nose to her throat; it sniffed her. What did it smell? Shea butter, coconut oil, her perfume, and beneath it all, her blood and fear, pumping fast and hot in her veins.

Elsie knew, even before it unhinged its jaw, that the creature would bite her. Still, knowing about violence, bracing for and expecting pain couldn't compare to experiencing it. Practice, theory—they stood apart, distanced as an estranged family. Elsie braced and braced, and when the thing bit her, she howled. It tore her, tore into her. It ripped at her throat like a wild dog. The creature was starved, ruthlessly and desperately so, and all Elsie could do was kick her feet, choke and gurgle through the geysers of blood bursting from her neck.

There was nothing like it, the pain. Elsie remembered breaking her arm as a child, the singular white-hot pain that had shot through her, but it was nothing in comparison to this. This pain was total, complete; there was no escape. Elsie stretched her body out long, stretched her toes and fingers wide, stretched away from the pain. Her blood—her *blood*—pumped out and out.

How long was she there in that hallway? How long was she spread flat on that horrible, dingy carpet, bleeding and twisting, and begging for help, for God, for death? Maybe minutes, maybe hours.

Elsie closed her eyes. Maybe if she submitted, the thing would let her go, let her die. She thought of Erika expecting her text at any moment, of Yvonne calling out for her to be safe.

Be safe, be safe, but how could anyone ever guard against this?

*

The neighbor who found Elsie wasn't any of the ones she

knew by name. A standoffish woman, a little cold and fussy about noise—she told the police that she'd thought Elsie had some man over.

"I thought she was seeing some guy. Had my volume turned up to twenty-something, all that screaming and carrying on."

She also thought Elsie was dead when she found her. There was hardly anything left of her—more gore than girl. Her dress was in shreds; body bare, bruised and gashed. Her flesh—and she was all flesh—was scored like bread dough. Her eyes were glossed over, her brown skin nearly translucent. When the neighbor had gotten close enough to check if Elsie had a pulse ("I'm a registered nurse, though I don't like to work at home"), she was both happy and horrified to hear Elsie's desperate, ragged breath.

"Her neck... I couldn't believe her neck." The nurse touched her throat and shuddered. "It was all black and crusted over. Nasty. I thought some wild dog had come in and ate her."

This Elsie heard afterward, in the hospital. She noticed guests only vaguely and through a thick beaded curtain of pain killers. Doctors and nurses filtered in and out, an endless procession of white and blue. The nurse-neighbor (she introduced herself, finally, as Miss Franklin) brought updates from the apartment, from medical staff. Yvonne and Erika appeared at her bedside with piteous looks, tears and gifts.

Elsie, for her part, moved little and spoke even less. Her voice was hoarse, ruined; she called only for water, and, when she was well enough, unsalted crackers.

By the end of her month-long stay, Elsie's room was crowded with balloons, cards, teddy bears and flowers, but Elsie saw nothing, wanted nothing. Erika took her home, eyeing her nervously from the driver's seat.

"You sure you don't want me to come up? Help you get settled?"

Elsie shook her head, leaped from the car the moment Erika rolled to a stop in front of her building.

"Call me if you need anything, me or Yvonne. Any time, sis, we'll be here." But Elsie was already past the gate, fast-walking her way through the complex's door.

If someone was viciously attacked and the world spun on without pause, did the attack even happen? Either no one in the complex save for Miss Franklin knew, or they all knew and couldn't be bothered. Elsie wasn't sure what was worse—ignorance or feigned ignorance. Either way, Elsie walked to her apartment in dead silence.

At her door, the truth was undeniable. Someone, Miss Franklin or one of her friends, had laid down a "Welcome" mat to hide the discolored carpet, but the bloodstain was just too big. It spread, brown and crusty, stinking vaguely of carpet cleaner and bleach. Elsie pictured Miss Franklin coming to scrub the blood from off the floor after a long shift, and was stricken with horror, shame and guilt.

She stepped over the rug, the stain. Stepped into her apartment, which she hadn't seen in weeks. Nothing felt the same as it did, everything was twee and dull and unfamiliar. It felt like she was walking through a stranger's house, picking up random objects and putting them down, wondering about the smallness of the rooms. Even her things, her precious curios and handpicked furniture, felt like clutter.

"Right," said Elsie aloud. She spoke to herself, to the apartment. "That's done, that's over. The end."

She'd already decided, a week and a half after the attack, that it wouldn't own her. It couldn't own her, not ever. Every so often that single-minded terror crept in on her, and Elsie had to grab onto her brain, lay it flat and talk it down. *Worse things have happened*, she told herself. *It doesn't matter, it can't matter. See, you've already forgotten it, all those things you can't even name. Mind over matter. It never happened if I can't remember it, if all my memories of that night slip like water through my fingers.*

And so, she went on. Elsie returned to work and went out with her friends, laughed and took her pain medication, journaled and exercised and did yoga and cut out caffeine and threw herself into her job.

Still. But.

164

Something in her, something in the very core of her being had changed. She was no longer Elsie-From-Before—only Elsie-After, and Elsie-After was deeply and permanently scared. Scared of noise, scared of strangers, scared of quiet, scared of friends. Before, Elsie thought fear was something she could control like dancing or eating or sleeping, but it was formless, everywhere, in her and on her. She slept with the lights on, started turning down nighttime invitations. Crowds unsettled her, but so too did being alone. Noises and movement, slight or big, startled her into tears. Elsie learned to fear her shadow.

She tried breathing through it, tried rationalizing herself out of what she felt, but the damage was done.

*

The streets she once adored sickened her. Elsie hated her apartment, hated the city. Who were all those people out there? Elsie didn't know those men at the corner store, couldn't name even one of the vagrant teens. Erika tried, Yvonne tried. Even Miss Franklin tried, but there was absolutely no luring Elsie out.

What could she tell them? How could she explain it? She stopped answering her phone, ignored the door. Letters and food piled up on her doormat. Her voicemail could take no more messages.

Inside, inside, Elsie was changing. Her rose-colored glasses were bleary with blood, and she no longer believed in the inherent goodness of people. What a piece of work was man, indeed! How vicious in deed! In action, how much like beasts. Paragon of animals, her ass—a rabid dog would've at least had the decency to kill her instead of leaving her to bleed out slow and alone.

Her mind darkened, became mazy and strange, twisting and untwisting upon itself. She looked out her window and seethed, angry with the world for turning even as she suffered, and angrier with herself for suffering. What *was* this? Elsie couldn't make sense of her nightmares, her terrors, her spiraling thoughts which took her down and down into the depths of herself, pinned her back onto the brown carpet.

She wanted to hurt something—herself, someone else, anything. She stopped bathing; she reeked, sometimes, of copper or spoiled meat. Her jaw cracked unpleasantly—her teeth fell out one by one, and grew back longer and sharper, her canines protruding from her mouth like fangs.

Elsie, she who once adored sunlight and parks and beaches, learned to loathe the sun. For days on ends, she kept to the dark, still quiet of her apartment, and tried to remember the face of the thing that attacked her.

(She saw it, once—it stood in her bathroom mirror, dead-eyed, oblivious to being watched, mimicking her every gesture.)

Elsie ate nothing, stopped sleeping. She calcified, putrefied; rotted. For three months, she sequestered herself. For three months, she saw no one and heard nothing. She supped on the vermin that moved in with her; huge rats, ants and palmetto bugs.

Her nails became like talons, and hair had grown long and matted. Solitude made her strange; she lost her taste for language, scuttled and scrambled around on all fours.

Sometimes, rarely, Elsie looked out her window and saw the world. Her mouth watered at the sight of the people. Brown-red saliva drooled down her chin. She was hungry, wasn't she? For food, yes, but also for company. She missed her friends, missed their talk and mannerisms, even as she couldn't recall their names or faces.

So, she went out. Outside, outside, into all that noise and commotion, light and color. It was chaos; it was beautiful. She stood outside the bright, gorgeous places she used to frequent and mourned her loss of them, of herself. It was a fabulous night full of awesome and awful noise. Everyone was so beautiful, so happy, so pleased to be out, to be in good company. What a piece of work was—

She. The moment Elsie laid eyes on her, her heart stopped in her chest. She was so lively, so bubbly and shiny. The sequins on her dress flashed attractively underneath the street lamps; blue and pink and purple, swishing

167

around her legs. If there was any sort of evil in the world, the girl was immune to it. All that touched her was good and sweet. All she saw was youth and light, the comfort of community. Besides, what could happen to her? The world was her friend, and it would hold her as it always did. Her friends told her to be safe, and so she would be.

Elsie watched the woman click by, following behind at a distance. She lived not far from Elsie's, alone in a little condo with just a gate to separate city from safety. They might've been friends some other time, Elsie and this girl, if Elsie hadn't been so hungry.

But the girl was pretty and alive, a light show in a party dress. Maybe Elsie would follow her for a little while longer, just up the stairs and down the hall, too dim for such a pretty dress. Maybe Elsie would get close enough to smell her, her body butter and perfume.

For now, though, Elsie only followed.

Niecey's Garden

Niecey, Niecey, quite contrary,
How does your garden grow?

Certainly, it wasn't a typical garden. Niecey grew no produce, cultivated no fruits or vegetables or flowers. Squash and tomatoes bored her, and roses had no smell to her. She was unmoved by the sight of bluebells, bonnets, nor did she swoon over the colors of hydrangeas, cornflowers and carnations. Phlox and cockscomb, lovely as they were to others, inspired no joy in Niecey.

No, what she loved best, what she preferred above all other growing things, was fungi. Common mushrooms, shiitake mushrooms, hen-of-woods, turkey's tail, shaggy parasols, liberty caps, deer shields and lion shields, orange bonnets, dripping bonnets, fairy ring mushrooms, enoki, that wide and varied motley of fungi that were not technically mushroom but were enough alike to be classified alongside them. Niecey had an extensive collection of puffballs and stinkhorns, polypores and chanterelles, earth stars and smuts. The back of her house was a shrine to decay, a love story written in spores. By day, her lawn and backyard were bright with scarlet elf cups and wrinkled peaches, delicate little entoloma hochstetteri—a sea of reds and browns, creams and whites, purples and blues accentuated by caps of yellow and green. Come nighttime, her garden glowed, the bioluminescent fungi burning blue-green and bright, their phosphorescence shining in the dark like so many neon eyes. And the smell of it—oh, how Niecey adored the scent of her garden! It was the very stink of things being eaten, things being made anew. How earthy it was, musty and rich as petrichor. If she could bottle it, that smell that coated the lining of her throat like a slime, she'd drink it.

The best part of the garden was near the chain-link fence that sat all the way at the back of her land. She found it two months after moving into the place, quite literally stumbling into it, tripping on a root and falling into a patch of unfamiliar mushrooms. A check of her handy field guide told her that the cluster of white-and-brown gilled caps were destroying angels, amanita ocreatea. Learning of their toxicity only made them more attractive to her. They were divine, these perfect little cherubs bursting from their veils, stretching languorously over her garden floor. Niecey saw how close they were to her edible mushrooms—the amanita velosa, the cremini and portobello—and felt a curious pressing on her chest. It would be so easy to make a mistake, to confuse the white stipe of a common mushroom with that of a poisonous one. Niecey traced her fingers along the gilled undersides of the destroying angels depicted in the field guide, shuddering.

She walked in the garden now, slow and lazy after a long day of work, her cardigan pulled closed against the chilly spring air. Though Niecey much disliked those people who dismissed all human lives as meaningless, she did feel that there was nothing on earth that understood her more deeply than her fungi. With people, there were all sorts of expectations and standards, social cues she had to obey, looks and subtexts she was meant to decipher. People were noisy, constantly chatting, constantly looking at her, or if they weren't, they didn't like when she looked at them, all focused and intent, trying to understand how they held themselves, what it meant when they said this or that thing. With other human beings, Niecey was not just Niecey—she was weird, an outsider. She stared too much, talked too little, fidgeted and twitched, went on and on and on about things that no one else cared for, had not enough to say about things that "mattered". Niecey did try to fit in, but she stuck out, a witches' butter in a sea of morels.

In her garden, surrounded by her fungi, Niecey was just another organism, a thing that breathed and ate and slowly decayed. She was what she was, not bound to any sort of human ideal of attractiveness or usefulness, and then, someday, she'd die. Niecey stood in the midst of her mushrooms. She was simply Niecey, alive and existing and there.

Huffing softly through her nose, Niecey squatted down beside a fallen cedar branch. It was beginning to break down, the flesh being stripped away by her little decomposing friends. She poked at it with her bare index finger. There were new spores budding around it, and a slow marching trail of fire ants were making their way over the branch. She leaned in closely, skin itching and crawling at the sight of crawling things, strange but not unpleasant. Niecey swatted at her arm without looking and sank her knees deeper into the earth.

Her birthday was soon, only two weeks away. Niecey, never quite interested enough in time and celebrations, thought a little about what she'd like to do for herself. She was friendless, had no family; the people she knew from her office job might've pooled together their money to buy her a cake if they knew her birthdate, but Niecey kept to herself and resisted all attempts to be known. Usually, she spent her birthdays on her lonesome, treating herself to a dinner, a nice dessert or a new book. There was nothing wrong with her routine, but it was her thirtieth birthday, a milestone. It would be nice to do something different.

Running her fingers through the lush soil, dark dirt sifting through her brown fingers, Niecey wished, not for the first time, that she could be closer to the earth she held. She wished she was an ant, a new green sprout, or even a worm. She'd be free from the human fears of aging, the panic over wrinkles and weakening bones. If she were a tree, thousands and thousands of years old, her age would be nothing but thin rings, round and round in an endless spiral. She'd grow tall, sweep the clouds with her leaves and, in time, break and fall and rot, becoming food for the saplings who in turn would grow and fall.

Alas, Niecey was flesh and bone and muscle; age meant wrinkled skin, time come and time gone, people born and people dead, the years passing her by at a breakneck speed. Time meant burying all those who mattered to her, and staying lonely so she'd never have to say goodbye. And what was so great about living anyway, Niecey wondered. In the end, she'd die and feed her beloved earth. Living, aging, it only prolonged the inevitable.

It came to her then, finally, what she'd do for her thirtieth birthday. Her heart pounded in her chest as she considered it, the dirt falling through her fingers as her hands numbed and slackened. For this birthday, her final birthday, she'd go into the earth. No more waiting, no more patiently biding her time. Niecey would give herself over to her garden.

The thought of it dizzied her, and all throughout the evening, Niecey argued with herself, against her dying, for her dying. But what about her books, she'd ask herself, and she'd answer that most books bored her anyway, none of the people depicted at all relatable. What about my friends, my family? What friends, thought Niecey. And what family? Everyone you ever loved died long ago. Niecey slipped into bed and folded her hands over her chest, trying to imagine what it would be like to be dead. Darkness, surely, and rot and the knowledge that she was no more.

How would she do it, if she did do it? Would she cut herself, gut herself? Would there be blood? Or would she off herself with pills, rat poison, bleach or laundry detergent? Niecey drifted off to sleep uneasily, her dreams green with her own decomposing body. She was laid in her grave, bloated and stinking, the animals and insects burrowing into her guts, gorging themselves on what remained of her. By the end, she was nothing but bones, fleshless, her teeth being all that distinguished her.

*

Upon waking, Niecey had her solution—mushrooms. It was so obvious and natural. Such violences as shooting herself or tearing at her wrists promised blood, but there was no promise she'd end up in the garden. A neighbor might get curious about the noise and call the ambulance, her birthday ruined by the bleach smell of the hospital. And manmade toxins were no better. If she did get into the garden, the bile in her body could easily harm her precious fungi. Yes, the mushrooms were the only way. The kingdom of God was within her because she ate it—the kingdom of fungi did too.

*

To put her affairs in order was to remove all the things that tied her to life. Niecey didn't have many. She was an only child and had buried her Ma and Dad years ago. She didn't know the people at her job well, nor did she make friends easily. People passed through her, and for once, her rootlessness was a relief. A lack of connections, personal or otherwise, meant there would be no one to mourn her, no one to search for her body and weep over her bones. To be alone was to control it all. To control it all was to have peace at last.

The first thing Niecey did was return her library books. She had four out—a Margaret Atwood book of poems, two Jane Austen novels, and a book on rare mushrooms. She wasn't comfortable with her corpse having debts, and she didn't like the idea of people at the local library scouring the shelves for *Emma* and *Mansfield Park* only for them to be gathering dust on her table. So, she took the books back, and walked through the stacks before returning home. She took nothing, though she did flip through a botany book and made note of a few recipes from a French cookbook.

Niecey considered quitting her job, but decided against it. Surely such a sudden change would alarm people to her plans. She didn't want people fussing over her. She continued on with her daily routine, going to work, making no waves, speaking very little, and, after leaving the office, arranging her death.

Those final days were filled with preparations, shopping for and buying up anything she thought might sweeten her last supper. She purchased a lovely green chinoiserie tureen along with a matching bowl at an antique store, two new sets of sheets (she expected to need changes, what with the gastrointestinal distress), a pink glass vase, a bronze candelabra, an antique zippo lighter, and a vast assortment of bath oils and soaps.

The following Monday, a week before her birthday, Niecey washed and plaited her hair, dressed in her second favorite dress (blue gingham, tulle under the skirt), and went to work for the final time. Single-mindedly she handled her tasks, typing meaningless numbers, writing countless emails. When her co-workers made and laughed at jokes she couldn't understand, Niecey laughed along with them. She made an effort in the breakroom to be sociable, sitting with the others as she ate her sandwich from home. And later, when she had clocked out, Niecey made empty promises to a few of her co-workers to go out with them next Friday, to go dancing or drinking, to be young.

"Anyways, Niecey, isn't it your birthday soon?" said one of the women.

Niecey smiled and nodded. "Yes. Thank you so much for remembering."

Afterwards, Niecey went to the grocery store and bought all the ingredients she needed for her birthday meal. She'd settled on a mushroom soup recipe she found online, something thick and creamy with lots of hearty chunks of mushroom. As she rattled and squeaked down the aisle, she caught sight of a flower display. She chose a bouquet of hydrangeas, their long stems bound together by a rubber band.

At home, Niecey picked her mushrooms. When her little basket overflowed with destroying angels and death camas, vomiters (chlorophyllum molybdites), she took them inside and sautéed them with wild garlic and butter. The smell was heavenly, overwhelming in her galley kitchen. Then came the flour, the salt and pepper, the fancy brand of chicken broth she had splurged on. She mixed the soup slowly, a little amazed as the ingredients merged into one smooth and fragrant whole. Niecey's mouth watered.

For a while, Niecey wondered whether she shouldn't bathe first then set the table, or do the opposite, set the table then bathe. In the end, she decided to have her bath first, filling up her small tub with bubble bath and oils, languishing in the perfumed water until her fingers pruned. As she washed (a sweet-smelling soap she bought on a whim from a department store, crushed lilacs or roses), she thought a little more on how she'd die. It would be painful and miserable and horrible, but God what a relief! She dunked herself into the water. It would feel like this, thought Niecey, like being under and underneath. She stayed down for as long as she could, and when she came up again, she found herself disappointed she couldn't stay for longer.

Next came the table setting. She put a lot of thought into it; she wanted a spectacle, something grand for her last supper. Already, Niecey had prepared a playlist, a clever mix of pop songs and somber music scores. She used a lacy, moth-bitten curtain as a table cloth and set her place with an embroidered cloth napkin, a spoon, and a glass of spring water. The soup, having been warming on the stove all through her bath, was poured into the green tureen, then placed on the table alongside the candelabra and the blue vase holding the blue hydrangeas. She put her bowl, fragile bone china embossed with Mandarin characters, in its place, started her playlist and lit her candles.

She knew she was teasing herself now, winding herself up. Her stomach was tight with excitement, with nerves. Niecey's hands trembled as she served herself the soup, the steam from the tureen making her face damp. She couldn't wait—she wanted all of it, every single toxic drop, to lick the bowl and clean the spoon, her stomach full of destroying angel and fool's mushroom, deadly conocybe and funeral bell. Her breath shuddered out of her as she smoothed the cloth napkin over her lap, sniffed the soup, and then, finally, took a bite.

It was a very tasty poison, not at all bitter or dangerous tasting. Spoonful after spoonful, Niecey ate, almost greedily, slurping down the onion and thick chunks of mushroom. Those alone were delicious—the flavor of them, the butter and seasoning, the earthy taste. Niecey moaned around her spoon, stopping only to sip her water or dab at her mouth. At the final bites, Niecey slowed, savoring those final morsels, rolling the mushrooms around her tongue.

Afterwards, Niecey cleaned her kitchen. It wouldn't do to have her house a mess, even postmortem. Her ghost, confined as her decomposing body would be to the ground, would surely be annoyed at the sight of her home in disrepair. And, because dead things couldn't load dishwashers, Niecey washed and dried the dishes, mopped the floors, cleaned out the tub, made and re-made her bed, dusted the wood surfaces and polished the metal ones. She went out in the garden, out among the mushrooms which she'd soon become one with, to water the grass and spread compost. She thought of how soon she'd be compost.

She wasn't tired yet. She checked the clock—just a little after ten in the evening. Niecey rested on the couch, flipping through a book on fungi and listened to what remained of her playlist. Bored, listless and impatient, Niecey went through each room making last minute adjustments to her things. Well, not her things, anymore. It was just stuff now, purposeless trinkets without an owner. The thought of the furniture going to waste bothered Niecey, so she took a few blank sheets of paper and detailed all that she wanted done with the place. Not a will—no, a will felt so dreary, and the writing of it morose, even in the shadow of her death—and certainly not a suicide note. This, all of this, this whole plan, none of it was suicidal. It was more like a homecoming; earth returning to earth, the disturbing human form falling back into the soil from which it was formed. Niecey couldn't imagine just who would find her letter—the mailman, maybe—but she sealed it in an envelope, and set it on her porch.

Finally, she was beginning to feel sleepy. Niecey retired to her room, her dreams mossy, sweet with the taste of mushroom.

The first day of dying was painless enough save for one or two strong stomach spasms. Niecey called in sick, her pained voice not at all affected as she told the lady from HR that she must've picked up a stomach bug. She said she didn't know when she'd be back in, and spent the rest of her day in repose, queasy but otherwise fine.

The second day proved the gastrointestinal ruining powers of the destroying angel. She had had food poisoning just once in her life. She remembered the vomiting, the shitting, the dry heaving and aura of sickness that radiated from her. This was worse, her stomach fighting anything and everything she tried to give it. Every sip of water, every nibble of cracker sickened her. Just moving too quickly turned her stomach, had her rushing to the bathroom to relieve herself.

On the third day, Niecey stumbled into her bedroom, laid herself down and stopped trying to fight the poison. She was ashamed of the way she'd behaved the day before, proud and determined, eating and drinking and carrying on with living as if she wasn't meant to be hollowing herself out. The body, devoted to life, accustomed to breathing, resisted what the mind knew needed to be done. It was like when she was younger, holding her breath to spite her mother, only to discover how resistant her body was to

181

dying. Now, though, grown and unwavering in her journey towards death, she submitted. Strengthened by her new promise to die with dignity, Niecey set her head on her pillow and stared up at the ceiling, tracing the cracks as she soiled herself again and again. Soon enough there was nothing left in her, no bile or spit, not even trapped air. The room reeked, the sheets foul with dark, dehydrated urine and bilious vomit and feces. Niecey spasmed, set her head back down and thought only of the end to her suffering.

By the fourth day, her stomach was calm again. It was, as Niecey knew, the false recovery stage when the body appeared to be healing just before the final death knells. She used the time to bathe herself and change the sheets before eating a small lunch of tea and crackers. She ran her hands over her skin, found it dry and scaly as a newt's. Niecey came in and out of consciousness, one moment aware of her mission and the next moment confused. She understood her illness; she could not understand why the world was spinning. She remembered everything; she remembered nothing. Niecey moved through her rooms, dizzy, detached from her body, feeling very much that she'd already left the earth. Her body was an empty vessel and she was above it, hovering over it, watching this other Niecey stare blankly at walls and supervising it as it wandered outside to touch its dry hands to the lichen. Who was this creature? Surely, they were not even of the same breed. The Niecey she knew was spry and fastidious; this thing in the garden was listless, distracted, rolling her eyes and grinding her teeth. And Niecey, strong and impenetrable Niecey, did not faint, weak from hunger, crashing her delicate head to the floor and falling waiflike into chairs and against walls. She tried to merge the strong and weak versions of herself in her mind, and her mind bucked against her. It would not show her her thoughts as they once were—clear and analytical—but as horrors, green and vicious from beneath the earth.

That night and next morning, delirium set in. Her body bisected, shattered. She saw her mother and father come back from the grave to frown at her deteriorating form. The walls fell away then the ceiling, and Niecey looked out into the outside and saw the world for what it was really was. Colors, just horrible colors and horrible visions. Niecey saw the smog, the vile streams of tainted water, the hordes of locusts devouring the earth. She saw the first woman being shaped from clay, and saw herself as the lining of her cocoon, watched as Lilith melted and reformed. Sick and healthy, caught in hell yet feeling closer to God than she ever had, Niecey witnessed the end times, the boiling bloody oceans and the stars dropping like hail from the heavens. Sirius pierced her chest as it plummeted into the sea and she screamed, half religious ecstasy and half mind-numbing pain.

The world was green and acid yellow, the buildings bioluminescent. Her garden bloomed inside of her, chewed hungrily at her organs. If there was any pain, Niecey was too far gone to register it. The seizures, the blood pooling in her brain, the terrible clenching in her stomach—what were these save for the suffering of the flesh? And she was no longer flesh. No, Niecey was fertilizer, mulch, decomposed body meant to feed the planet. Niecey gazed dreamily at the nightmares that swaddled her. She would join them, she would join them now.

On the final day, the seventh day, Niecey used the last of her strength to rinse her skin, changed her clothes and walked out into the garden of fungus. It was her birthday, she was thirty years old. She tried to image her life in a series of photographs, a film, but saw only splotches of black. Was she born? Was she held? When her mind gave no answers, Niecey let go and went to her poison patch.

Lovely place to perish, held warmly by the vomiters and galerinas, the digestible but irritating emetic russulas and yellow stainers. Come summertime, the sun would shine hot and blazing on her corpse. She laid herself down and looked up at the sky, clear and lovely. A cool breeze passed her face. Niecey was little more than nerve endings, stomach boiling and face dripping with sweat, reeking and bruised, hideous, and yet she was so alive, so clean and fresh. She was needed now, and connected. Every inch of her body was supplementing the ground she lay on. Ants crawled over her, worms curled around her toes. The plants, her garden of death, took her in, housed her. Niecey saw the earth open up for her, the soil making a warm bed for her to sleep in. *Come in, come in*, it said, and Niecey went to it, to the place where she was always meant to be.

Niecey breathed. Niecey breathed no longer.

About the author

Yah Yah Scholfield is a writer of horror and speculative fiction. Their work has been featured in Fiyah Lit Magazine, as well as several other anthologies. In 2022, they published their debut novel *On Sundays, She Picked Flowers*. When they're not terrifying innocents, they're working as a professional stay-at-home daughter and wrangler of their cats, Chihiro and Sophie.

Milton Keynes UK
Ingram Content Group UK Ltd.
UKHW020211161223
434414UK00009B/49